MW00627084

# MAN-EATER
## BOOK THREE OF
## MURPHY'S LAWLESS

Griffin Barber

Beyond Terra Press
Virginia Beach, VA

Copyright © 2020 by Griffin Barber.

All rights reserved. No part of this publication may be reproduced, distribut-
ed or transmitted in any form or by any means, including photocopying,
recording, or other electronic or mechanical methods, without the prior
written permission of the publisher, except in the case of brief quotations
embodied in critical reviews and certain other noncommercial uses permitted
by copyright law. For permission requests, write to the publisher, addressed
"Attention: Permissions Coordinator," at the address below.

Chris Kennedy/Beyond Terra Press
2052 Bierce Dr.
Virginia Beach, VA 23454
http://chriskennedypublishing.com/

Publisher's Note: This is a work of fiction. Names, characters, places, and
incidents are a product of the author's imagination. Locales and public
names are sometimes used for atmospheric purposes. Any resemblance to
actual people, living or dead, or to businesses, companies, events, institu-
tions, or locales is completely coincidental.

Cover Design by J Caleb Design.

Edited by Charles E. Gannon

Ordering Information:
Quantity sales. Special discounts are available on quantity purchases by cor-
porations, associations, and others. For details, contact the "Special Sales
Department" at the address above.

Man-Eater/Griffin Barber -- 1st ed.
ISBN: 978-1648550263

*For The Rainmaker: my thanks for all the opportunities you have created for me, not least of which is this very book.*

*Yours,*

*Griffin Barber*

# Book Three
# Man-Eater

By Griffin Barber

# MISSION LOG

UPDATE, MISSION DAY 046
MAJOR R.Y. MURPHY, CO, RECORDING

SUMMARY AO DATA, 55 TAURI B 3 (R'Bak)
LOCAL YEAR: 672 SR (Date coding note: SR stands for "Since Rev."
Origin of "SR" uncertain. Could refer to spaceside locals' first official recording of years (i.e., revolutions around the local star),
the political revolts that compelled the SpinDogs to leave R'Bak,
or the founding of their first rotational habitat, or rohab.)
LOCAL DATE: Day 049 (of 369) (Time sync note: Local days are
only 18 hours. Consequently, the local year of 369 days is actually only 75 percent the duration of one Earth year.)
EARTH DATE: August 31, 2125 AD

PREOP/STRATEGIC SITREP (approximate):
Increasing competition among powers in the primary system (Jrar)
may have prompted several nations on the main planet (Kulsis)
to move up the timetable on exploitation of R'Bak during the
imminent Searing. First mission arrived in this system (secondary star, Shex) 18 months earlier than on any previous Searing.
ELINT and SIGINT both indicate that the OpFor is from Kulsis'
second largest power, which has an entente/détente relationship with the greatest/oldest/traditionalist power.
Due to OpFor's early arrival at R'Bak, SpinDog and RockHounds
(two different branches of the spaceside local population) had
neither instituted full cessation of travel nor completed re-
concealment of stationary assets. Many were compelled to go
into hiding wherever they were, including various resource col-
lection teams on the second planet, V'dyr, and one trade mission concluding business on R'Bak.

MISSION DAY UPDATES
000 Ship carrying Lost Soldiers (Dornaani hull *Olsloov*) arrives in
system, scans, discovers SpinDogs on far side of local sun
(Shex). Observes, decodes comms. Language is quickly identi-

fied as a devolved form of Ktor as it was spoken almost 1,400 years ago (approximation only). Despite linguistic roots, *Olsloov* command staff deems it unlikely that the SpinDogs would become aggressive or that they have had any recent contact with the Ktoran Sphere.

001 Contact made by *Olsloov* command staff. Purpose: acquire consumables.

002 No response, but Spin/Rock ships move to avoid further LoS/lascom messages. Pickets of harvesters/raiders notice movement of the previously undetected Spin/Rock craft, begin maneuvering at extremely high gee (often 2–3, sustained) to effect intercept. Terran cadre analyzes the situation; *Olsloov* selectively jams OpFor broad-comms. Only transmission completed by OpFor was decrypted as "Investigating local anomaly; stand by for details." Narrow-beam comms blocked by position of companion star (Shex), which occluded receivers located in the primary (Jrar) system.

003 Sensor results from *Olsloov* indicate that OpFor's hi-gee maneuvers are consistent with a) intercept of SpinDog craft and b) repositioning to clear transmission coordinates to Jrar. Capt. Mara Lee, USAF, is restored from cryogenic suspension to assist in battlefield support and liaison duty with SpinDog matriarchy.

004 Contact established with Spin/Rock leadership using Dornaani translation system to update language from classic Ktor and to crack cyphers. Agreement reached. Compromised Spin/Rock craft adjust course to flee toward prearranged coordinates in outer system. Intercept trajectory for OpFor intersects optimal ambush point for *Olsloov* and her drones/ROVs. Captain Lee receives partial accelerated training in local language via virtuality immersion.

006 OpFor pursuit elements ambushed by *Olsloov* at edge of outer system. Tech superiority of *Olsloov* and her deployed assets results in complete elimination of enemy hulls without loss or significant damage. In and near R'Bak orbit, Dornaani ROVs (with direct oversight from Captain Lee) assist Spin/Rock assets to eliminate small number of OpFor hulls (mostly interface

transports) and sensors. Dornaani standoff drones eliminate two planetside comm arrays with potential to reach Jrar system.

007 *Olsloov* arrives on-station at R'Bak, conducts close survey for further planetside comm facilities with inter-system capability. None located. AARs generated and shared between *Olsloov* and Spin/Rock cadres.

008 Data sharing and first meetings between *Olsloov* and Spin/Rock leadership. Mutual support and joint operation agreements reached. Captain Lee is debriefed by *Olsloov* cadre and resumes accelerated language training via virtuality technology.

009 Transfer of volatiles and other consumables to *Olsloov* commences. Captain Lee completes accelerated language training.

010 Data packets for tech sharing and replication of 20th century Earth weapons and systems relayed to and declared operational by Spin/Rock automated production facilities. Examples of each system are provided from legacy examples carried aboard *Olsloov*. Legacy examples include helicopters, weapons, ammunition, simple electronics. Captain Lee commences training of first class of SpinDog rotary wing pilots.

013 Major RY Murphy restored from cryogenic suspension. Debrief commences.

014 Major Murphy debrief ends. Light company of Lost Soldiers detached for R'Bak ops is revived.

015 R'Bak ops contingent (Lost Soldiers) commences accelerated language training aboard *Olsloov*. *Olsloov* and seeded (permanent) microsat net detect upswing in movement by advanced vehicles on surface of R'Bak.

016 First planetside training sorties of SpinDog RWP pilots led by Captain Lee. Planetside movement increase is confirmed as OpFor activity. Spin/Rock intel assessment is that they are gathering resources to secure optimum construction site for transmitter capable of reaching Jrar system.

017 Guildmother/Matriarch of leading Spin/Rock Family reported to *Olsloov* as MIA planetside on R'Bak while conducting undisclosed SAR ops in north polar extents. Capt. Lee is cleared for, and tasked to, effect recovery of Guildmother/Matriarch, attached personnel, and others requiring rescue.

018 Capt. Lee's recovery mission achieves objective while sustaining moderate casualties, but Guildmother/Matriarch had been mortally wounded prior to her arrival in AO.

019 *Olsloov* cadre, Lost Soldier CO Murphy, and SpinDog leadership agrees to conops of joint contact and recruitment mission to R'Bak. Objective: gather sufficient indigenous forces and commandeer cached Kulsis equipment to disrupt and prevent OpFor construction of dirtside inter-system comm array. Spaceside requirements articulated; assets identified. Preps begin. Construction of improvised meteoritic assault capsules commences, with limited assistance from Dornaani and contemporary Terrans. Mission leadership selected and briefed. Training commences.

021 Lost Soldier R'Bak detachment completes language training, skills assessment, physical readiness conditioning, and is officially stood up as an active unit. Designation pending.

022 *Olsloov* completes replenishment activities, prepares for departure. Training for joint mission to R'Bak concludes. Objectives and targets updated. Final briefing.

023 *Olsloov* departs.

024 Mission dropship commences op with tug boost toward R'Bak along retrograde orbital track.

028 Orbital insertion successful. Joint mission under command of Lt. Harold Tapper confirmed as maneuvering to establish contacts with Sarmatchani nomads.

036 SpinDog transport shuttles conduct high angle insertion to R'Bak north polar regions, followed by subsonic overland NOE flight to convey task force under Cpt. Hubert Moorefield to border of Hamain desert region in northern hemisphere. Cpt. Moorefield establishes and assumes command of Camp Stark FOB, proximal to anticipated rendezvous point with Lt. H. Tapper.

045 Lt. H. Tapper coordinates and conducts successful Sarmatchani strike against elements of J'Stull satrapy. Mission-critical Kulsian vehicle cache, along with relevant operational supplies, taken and being convoyed to elements from Camp Stark.

046 Seized vehicles and supplies are transferred to Cpt. Moorefield, CO Camp Stark, at rendezvous point. J'Stull pursuit/attack repulsed after suffering heavy losses. Abandoned and reclaimable equipment includes APCs, light ACVs, and company-level personal gear, including Kulsian small arms. Note: otherwise unbreakable draught creatures (*whinaalani*) allow themselves to be ridden by our personnel. Casualties: 11 WIA, 1 WIA/ND ("non-deployable"), 4 KIA.

\* \* \* \* \*

# Chapter One –
# Rolling Up

Chalmers was going too fast to do more than brace himself against the wheel as the herd of alien whinnies appeared in front of the speeding buggy as if by magic.

A cop he'd once known said that was what all the responsible parties said in car accidents: "The other car just appeared in front of me!" when they might have seen that shit coming if they hadn't been going too fast for the conditions.

He supposed the chest-high, six-meter-long, weighing-better-than-a-ton lizard-like creatures did not deserve the moniker "alien," at least not here, not on their home turf.

They certainly resented the buggy's sudden intrusion into their midst; a couple of the herd sounded a loud resonating threat-whistle while the others ran for it, scrambling up the side of the draw.

Chalmers tried for a clear spot in the herd, the big tires of the buggy spitting grit and gravel in their wake. He couldn't help but grin madly under the goggles. This was the most fun he'd had in almost two hundred years, for God's sake!

Then one of the whinnies feinted toward the nearest wheel, mouth open. The red-orange interior of the throat and finger-length opalescent teeth were all the encouragement he needed.

13

"Fast fuckers," Chalmers muttered, shifting gears and hammering the accelerator. He spent the next moment counter-steering against the shuddering skid he felt through the seat and wheel, then aimed for an opening in the rocks ahead.

They made it, but the gap ended up being a yard or so above the lower slope, and the buggy left the ground doing a feather under fifty.

They were airborne before Chalmers realized the animal—the freaking animal—had *feinted* an attack at the buggy, just like he used to mess with his stepmother's pissy old cats.

The landing pushed the buggy's occupants, both Terran and local, hard into their seats. The broad tires slipped before biting into the patchy turf of the uneven slope they bounced along. Chalmers adjusted his steering three times in as many seconds, fighting the inertia and momentum that threatened a roll-over. His efforts and the heavy-duty off-road suspension finally steadied the buggy, the uphill side compressing as the lower smoothly traveled to give them a more-or-less steady platform.

"Bastards know how to make a damn good buggy," Chalmers mused, taking a hand from the wheel to wipe something green-brown from his goggles.

"What?" Jackson shouted, his brown knuckles lighter where he clutched at the roll bars.

Chalmers would have to talk to Jackson about that. Chicken bars were there so you didn't lose digits holding onto the roll bars during a roll. It was yet another example of how little training they'd had before going on this mission.

But for now, Chalmers just shook his head, grinning madly behind his scarf as his downshift made the engine throb loudly. He'd been doing that a lot recently—smiling, not downshifting.

The rest of Murphy's people might grumble about all they'd lost, all that had been taken from them, but Ernest Earl Chalmers III had raised no fools. Chalmers chuckled, considering his brothers, and mentally qualified his statement: shitheads, maybe. Assholes, most definitely, but no fools.

He, more than any of the rest of the men and women stolen from their own times and places, was happy as hell to be anywhere but home. Sure, they might be at the ass-end of nowhere, but the fate he'd been facing at the end of the helicopter ride that had ultimately landed him here had well and truly sucked. Sucked bad enough to have made one Horace Earl Chalmers consider suck-starting a shotgun, truth be told.

"I'm too pretty for prison," Chalmers said. He glanced in the mirror at the well-equipped, by local standards at least, indig warrior riding in the rear passenger-side seat. Kenla was another example of the varied advantages this place and time had over Fort Leavenworth's prison: women.

"What?" Jackson repeated.

Chalmers raised his voice over the wind and engine noise. "How we doing for time?"

Jackson checked the pad in the hand he was not using to clutch the sissy bar. "Not bad, Chief!" he shouted. "So long as you don't wrap us around a tree, we're golden…" he continued, quietly enough that Chalmers could pretend he hadn't heard.

He glanced at the shiny display. The miniaturized computer was the only piece of SpinDog tech Chalmers had insisted their allies provide—well, it *and* a feed from the tiny spy sats crisscrossing overhead in whacky orbits. Seeded in advance of their arrival, the Dornaani satellites were almost entirely plastic—or something like it—and not much larger than a hubcap. Non-reflective and sheathed in some kind of temperature-equalizing material that made them thermally invisible, they sounded like something straight out of Area 51. If the locals did manage to detect them, though, they were reportedly programmed to take a swan dive into the atmosphere: burnt to ash in minutes. Still, Chalmers figured that if the opposing team found one, they'd look for more until the last one committed reentry suicide. And then the Lost Soldiers would be well and truly on their own.

But, hey, as long as they lasted, there was no way Chalmers was going to rely on barely remembered land navigation courses when his continued survival was on the line. Not when such wonders were available. Not on an alien planet with a different diameter and magnetic pole. GPS systems had first made an impression on him back in Desert Storm, and while Chalmers wasn't sure it operated on the same principles, this device was even more accurate and less bulky than what he had used back then. It was also easier to read—once you got used to the locals' cursive-meets-creep show writing.

He slewed the buggy around a stand of tree-sized plants that looked like a clump of insanely large blades of lawn grass pulled from the ground by a giant's shitty golf swing. Passing close enough to reach out and touch it, he realized the earthy clump at the base of the lawn grass was some kind of weird root-ball of dense-looking fibers.

The passenger directly behind him asked something like, "Fight wanted?"

Chalmers wasn't sure of the indig's name, just that he was the leader of the local resistance cell, and as such, was one of two "types." Either a guy with too much hero and too little common sense for his liking, or just another hopeful warlord in the making. Neither were high on Chalmers's list of people to hang out with, so Chalmers pretended not to hear the question.

Thoughts of warlords sent Chalmers on a trip down memory lane, remembering the big souk in Mogadishu, where you could buy anything, including some of yesterday's shipment of food, fresh off the UN relief trucks. These people had yet to prove themselves, so he wasn't about to go out on a limb for them. Because if he did, Murphy's Law made it a sure thing the locals would saw it off at the trunk. From the sticks, himself, Chalmers understood one immutable law of insular cultures: outsiders were afforded neither the respect nor care that insiders could rely on. He wasn't one of them, and there was no telling when they would decide to saw Chalmers' own shit off at the trunk if he did go out on limb for them.

"Fight wanted?" the indig repeated, loud enough that Chalmers couldn't ignore him without offending him.

"What's that?" Chalmers asked, working his way up through the gears as the way ahead became clear. They were still heading downhill toward where the valley debouched onto a wide floodplain crisscrossed with canals fed from a huge, shallow lake. The dry land between the waterways was the source of most of the local food production for the region. At least, that food which the nomads didn't herd through the mountains they were leaving behind. The village itself was visible now: twenty to thirty low edifices, water mill crouching on one edge of the largest, all surrounded by fields of ochre-green crop lands.

"You want fight, Warrant Officer?" the local repeated more loudly, emphasizing Chalmers' official title.

The locals were intensely rank conscious. It was almost as bad as the regular Army had been. Worse, even. Chalmers had no idea how to identify an indig's status at a glance. Not yet, anyway. He supposed he'd have to learn soon enough.

"I hope not." He slowed his speech, careful with his diction. "Not a straight fight, anyway. Want to get there and catch them with their pants down."

The male indig spoke equally slowly and carefully, clearly wanting to be understood. "Respectfully, then, may I ask you to slow, Warrant Officer Chalmers?"

"Why?"

"Because if you go fast, like raiders, they open fire. If they see me and Kenla, they less likely to shoot first, question later."

"Less?" Jackson said, jumping on the word before Chalmers could.

"Clarthu not friendly. Not all the time. We raid them from time to time. Nothing so bad to make them hate, but they not like a surprise."

Chalmers downshifted and let engine braking slow them. "I don't want to give the people we're looking for time to bail or hide their comms."

"Bail?" the indig war leader asked.

"Run away," Chalmers clarified. There were still some errors in translation, but the weird tech they'd been subjected to sure beat shit out of attending Defense Language Institute courses for months on end. Then again, DLI had been close enough to San Francisco to hit the clubs on weekends, so it had that going for it. Had. Very past tense. He hadn't even thought to ask if either place still existed.

The thought clawed at his sunny mood, disturbing his carefully cultivated cherub-like disposition. It made him question his level of comfort with the new world—worlds? universe?—that was his new reality.

"You agree?" the male asked as the buggy slowed.

"What?" Chalmers asked, memories of uncomfortable times slipping past his guard, carrying him off to revisit places and times he'd rather not have had to.

\* \* \*

**SPINDOG ROHAB (ROtational HABitat):**
**MISSION DAY 019**

"Rather not have to, Major," Chalmers said, carefully suppressing a flinch as Major Murphy snapped an angry stare his direction. He wasn't sure why he felt the urge to shy away. Murphy wasn't particularly imposing, and Chalmers knew that proper command authority to back Murphy's orders was, at the very least, way the fuck out of reach. Like, *light years* out of reach.

"What's that, Chief?" The major's tone was cool.

Upon learning just how lucky he'd been waking up here and now, Chalmers had taken a sober look at his life and the shit show it had become. In light of the messes he'd made in his life, Chalmers decided to do better. To *be* better. So, despite a strong natural inclination to tell the major some bullshit about being eager to take on the mission, Chalmers instead stuck to the course he'd charted for himself.

"With respect, Major, I'd rather not be dropped in the shit again. I mean, 'hearts and minds?' You've got operators for that. Hell, from what I hear, some of the men were around when the term was coined."

Murphy's tone chilled from unpleasantly cool to icy. "Warrant Officer Chalmers, I'm fairly certain I didn't ask what you'd rather. In fact, I'm certain I give not one fuck what you'd rather." The major paused, whether for effect or to prevent giving vent to his temper, Chalmers couldn't say.

Despite knowing the man lacked the legal authority to do much at all to him, Chalmers swallowed the disrespectful response that threatened to spill from his lips. His goal of being better was not going to just *happen*. No one was going to just hand Chalmers the respect he'd always craved. More important in this moment, Chalmers realized he actually gave a shit what this guy—what all the men—thought of him. He didn't like the mission, but Chalmers liked this man's contempt even less. And he wasn't sure what, exactly, he'd done to earn it.

Unless.

"Major, I apologize. I misspoke. W—"

"Did you?" Murphy snapped.

"My experience is almost exclusively CID," Chalmers explained. "Criminal investigation is my area of expertise. I've got no experience getting people to come around to our si—"

Murphy's waved Chalmers' protest down, his icy demeanor taking on the weight and majesty of a glacier as he leaned forward. "I don't need you to win their hearts and minds, Warrant Chalmers. I need you to investigate; to identify and root out the equivalent of a local crime ring and locate hidden caches of off-planet tech. You do have a proven track record of rooting out such networks, of properly identifying and seizing their contraband. Your selection for this mission was precisely due to certain moral ambiguities with which you seem perfectly comfortable, given the…activities that led to your presence on the helo that was taking you out of Mogadishu." Chalmers swallowed a protest, knowing it would be a lie. Desperately seeking to ingratiate himself—and not entirely sure why—he ventured, "I'd be careful, Major, about how much you reveal of people's backgrounds."

Murphy's wintry smile accompanied the confident regard of a man entirely indifferent to any leverage or bluster. "Is that a threat, mister?"

"Fuck, no, Major! I just meant—Look, I wasn't on my way home, but being transferred pending the results of their investigation. An already-completed investigation. Sending me out on orders was just a face-saving measure my CO and—" Murphy opened his mouth but Chalmers raised a hand, eyes pleading as he rushed on. "I know what I did. Here and now, I ain't denying it. But the information of what I did would only be available *after* we were shot down. You being in possession of that information tells a suspicious person you might be a participant in the program that kidnapped us. If you have similar information on others of us, you'll want to be careful about what and how you reveal it. I'm telling you, I've interviewed enough shitheads to know they're always looking to lay the blame for getting caught at someone else's feet. In this case—" he shook his head "—I know the rest of the soldiers aren't likely to be shits like me. But even for a straight GI-fuckin'-Joe, getting stuck in this whole fucked up situation is gonna feel like they 'got caught'…by something or someone. So, whatever you can do to keep people from automatically thinking you're part of that 'something or someone,' the better."

Murphy's right eye twitched, the only sign the major wasn't carved of ice. Then again, it actually looked more like an involuntary tic.

"I know you weren't party to it," Chalmers blurted, hands up in surrender. "I'm just saying, well, those 'Nam-era snakes did coin another term, something about, 'fragging COs.'"

Murphy blinked. Both eyes this time. Definitely not a tic. A moment passed. Another. The major's sharp nod was more the calving of an iceberg than anything resembling an acknowledgement that Chalmers might have a point. Or that he'd managed to thaw Murphy's disdain in the slightest.

"Frankly, I don't have any choice but to plug you in. If ever I discover you've jeopardized the mission—a mission intended to secure the survival of every single one of us—I will find a way to make certain you are put out of my misery. Besides, your ability to think around certain corners like that is just the turn of mind this particular mission requires, Chief. *If* you can stay on mission?"

Chalmers, noticing the major had resumed calling him by the honorific warrants were usually given, started breathing again. Not trusting his voice, he nodded mute understanding.

"Mission-specific briefing materials and your training schedule will be available after lunch. Language training begins tonight. Sergeant Jackson—I presume you'll want him—will join you once medically cleared. He'll have to play catch up."

"Shouldn't be a problem for him. He's a lot better at languages than me," Chalmers said, fighting a wave of relief that Jackson would be on his side again.

"Very good. Dismissed."

Chalmers stood, saluted, and left.

It was only when he started reading the briefing that Chalmers realized the mission was to take place in only a couple weeks. Despite the short timeframe, Major Murphy had acted as if they could reach a useful level of language competency in that time. Instead of whining to command right then and there, Chalmers read the rest of the briefing materials and in due time discovered just how Murphy thought they'd be up to speed.

Fucking unreal, the things the Doorknobs could do.

\* \* \*

### CLARTHU: MISSION DAY 052

The unreal nature of what they were doing slapped Chalmers as they approached the village.

It wasn't just the two suns overhead, though what a mindfuck that was! No, it was the whiplash between the familiar and the fucking out-there that was hard for Chalmers to process.

He'd come to this system on a fucking starship, spent a few weeks on a hab that was still decades ahead of the fevered imaginings of sci-fi writers of his own time, then boarded *another* spaceship (the SpinDogs had explained the difference between the two) to land on an alien world.

Then, after puttering around a camp not unlike the one where he'd been based in the Mog, he'd driven through mountains in a dune buggy. Both the buggy and the mountains wouldn't have been out of place in Baja California, though the flora and fauna were occasionally lobotomy-level reminders Chalmers wasn't in Kansas anymore, Toto. Then, in the mountains, Chalmers and Jackson had met with a bunch of nomads that resembled nothing so much as an egalitarian version of Kipling's Afghans.

Now, this village: straight out of *The Eagle Has Landed*, less the lush green hillsides of England's countryside and the uniformed military presence of that film. Then again, here the adults all carried weapons and the buildings were half-dug into the ground, but there was a water mill that reminded Chalmers of that film. Hell, if he tried hard enough, he could even reimagine the buggy as a jeep, and be whatshisname...the young US Army Captain who took down "zee Germans" and Michael Caine.

It all led to mental whiplash akin to some strange, bloodless version of what the Nam-era guys had gone through coming home.

"Just need a few years of catching up," Chalmers mumbled under his breath.

He dropped the buggy into first gear and slowed even further as they came into range of the big-bore weapons the indigs used. And there were armed men and women manning the earthen berm surrounding the village. Some had no doubt fled to the fields when they heard the buggy's snarling approach.

"What?" Jackson asked.

"Nothing, man. Just a moment of weird."

Jackson grunted and turned to look at their guides. The male indig unbuckled and stood up in the seat.

"The Kedlakis-Ur sends greetings and *something*," he shouted through cupped hands. "*Something* of the Kedlakis-Ur wish to meet with the hetman."

One of the guards, a tall, wasp-waisted woman, waved them on.

Chalmers kept the buggy at a walking pace as they crossed the last few yards to an opening in the berm. There was talk between some of the other villagers and the woman, but she mostly ignored it and waved them through the gap without any further discussion.

Chalmers, mildly astonished that a brief statement was all the villagers required to give them access to the village, almost caused the buggy to stall.

"You insisted on driving," Jackson said. "Least you could do is keep us from looking stupid in front of these people."

Chalmers just drove on, his head on a swivel.

A space Chalmers assumed was the equivalent of a village green lay just beyond the berm. A brief drive between low, adobe-brick buildings followed. They entered a small square with a well in the center and a larger building on the left.

"Stop there," the talkative guide said, pointing to the building opposite the large one.

An older, richly dressed man stood at the entrance, a fruit of some kind surrendering its skin to a wicked-looking knife wielded in capable hands.

Chalmers stopped the buggy and shut her down. The hot metal of the motor pinged as it cooled. Chalmers immediately felt the sweat, held in check by the wind of their passage, begin to run down his flanks.

"This is the village *something*, Larn Clarthu, Warrant Officer," their guide said, waving at the fruit-peeler.

Jackson, far better at languages than his partner, handled the niceties of the introduction, providing the SpinDog countersign.

Chalmers tried to act casual as he took stock of their surroundings. There were a couple of oldsters staring at them from around the well, but on the whole, the villagers seemed a lot less interested in their arrival than the nomads had been. There were some kids watching, sure, but they were chivvied back toward the fields and work abandoned in the excitement.

"The *somethings* will come," the hetman said, turning to enter what appeared to be his home.

Chalmers swallowed fears they were being set up and nodded at their guides. "Stay here, please?"

Both guides nodded, though there was something in the woman's body language Chalmers didn't like. His tolerance for things he didn't like had been mightily adjusted by circumstances, so Chalmers ignored the feeling and followed Jackson.

The half-underground lodge was cool after the growing midday heat, and carpets of some beautifully-dyed material softened sound and lent an air of civilization to what would otherwise be a spartan, cave-like dwelling.

The village hetman was a hard-looking fifty-ish. Thinking about it, Chalmers couldn't recall seeing an older indig, which fit the briefing. Namely, that those locals who didn't collaborate with R'Bak's elites lived neither well nor long. The SpinDogs had provided fairly good intel, but it wasn't updated often enough to give more than deep background and a few points of contact for their area of operations. As Chalmers had reliably found reason after reason to doubt the accuracy of every intelligence briefing he'd ever been party to, he was always on the look-out for those moments when reality matched the brief. Of course, just because the SpinDogs had given the straight dope on the lay of the land didn't mean they hadn't spun the shit out of the details.

The hetman likely wasn't the collaborator they were looking for, since the village seemed too far from any real center of power for it to be worth the cost of buying him.

Distance didn't mean they were safe, though.

"A lot like Mogadishu," Chalmers muttered.

Jackson shot him a look, but Chalmers waved him off.

The hetman asked something too quickly for Chalmers to understand.

"No, not yet," Jackson's answer was slow, and far easier to understand than the local's.

"Not yet what?" Chalmers asked.

"Not here to overthrow the satrap," Jackson clarified.

Chalmers smiled at the hetman, nodding slowly. "Not yet, anyway. We want to catch"—he sought the word a moment—"spies."

"No spies here," the hetman said. His tone was level, but his gaze hardened.

"I'm sure everyone in this village is super happy with leadership," Chalmers said, in English.

"What does he say, Leader-Of-Ten?" the hetman asked.

Jackson shrugged and lied easily. "He quotes a general."

The hetman's suspicious gaze eased.

Chalmers noted the reaction and stored it under useful confirmation of information the SpinDogs provided. Specifically, that the indigs were militant in a way that most of Earth circa 1990 AD had gladly forgotten.

"Did anyone leave town as we came in?" Chalmers asked.

"No one, War Technician," the hetman said.

Chalmers liked the man's translation of Warrant Officer into the local lingo and decided not to correct him.

"Did anyone ask to leave, Larn Clarthu?" Jackson asked, glancing at Chalmers.

Smiling and nodding encouragement, Chalmers watched the villager, decided that, even more than before, he was glad Jackson was so much better with languages.

Larn Clarthu didn't answer directly, but picked up an ancient-looking rifle that had been hiding among the cushions at his knee and stood with a fast, fluid grace. Chalmers dimly recalled that, in R'Bak's outback, place-names were often taken from the clan that held dominion over them, and a hetman's title wasn't hereditary but earned in battle.

"Come," he said, when he noticed the visitors had not followed suit.

Jackson got up with similar ease and gave a hand to help Chalmers to his feet. As much as the body armor they'd been issued in the Mog made getting up and down a pain in the ass, Chalmers wasn't about to give up the additional protection it offered.

The hetman gestured with a scarred hand for the off-worlders to follow.

"He look like Ked to you, too?" Jackson asked quietly, pointing with a stubbled chin at the retreating back of the hetman.

"Who?" Chalmers blurted before realizing his partner meant the male half of their indig guides. He shrugged. "I guess so, yeah. But then they're all bound to be cousins or some shit."

"No wonder you're so cool with them. I forget how you rednecks are all related," Jackson shot at him. The sergeant pushed his way through the heavy leather curtain covering the first dogleg of the entrance to the hetman's home.

Remembering his promise, Chalmers swallowed a shitty remark and followed past the tight corners. Initially he'd thought the construction was intended to restrict airflow and keep the interior cool, and it probably helped with that, but now Chalmers suspected the primary intent was as a choke point in the event of an attack.

He was rounding the final corner when someone outside started shooting.

\* \* \* \* \*

# Chapter Two –

# In Brief

"How many shots?" Chalmers asked, glancing from the display to the briefing officer.

"Most of their long arms are single-shot breech-action, but there are more advanced arms in production, and the collaborators don't have all of them."

Chalmers listened, but his attention was back on the display. A rifle-armed woman was belly-crawling toward what looked like a cross between a turkey and a toothy lizard: it was one freaky-looking predator. Despite the awkward appearance, however, it was *definitely* a predator. The opening of the video had shown the alien things chasing down and dispatching one of the woman's equally-alien looking livestock with a single bite to the back of the critter's short, muscle-bound neck.

Preoccupied, the bird-thing slashed the belly of its prey with one claw, then thrust its smooth head fully into the gaping wound.

Chalmers, aware of the mixed company, carefully did not verbalize the crack every soldier ever would make on seeing the images.

The woman in the display carefully rose to one knee, leveled her long rifle, and took aim while the thing had its head *inside* the other thing.

The predator withdrew its bloody maw, a massive piece of organ meat distending the scaled throat as strands of bloody tissue quivered and stretched all the way back into the wound cavity. It was easy to imagine the sound of that mouth snapping closed around a human victim, given how wide and powerful the man-eating jaws were.

The woman fired.

The thing seemed to flinch. The dun rocks behind it were suddenly painted with oddly-tinted blood.

The shooter wasn't watching. She was already reloading, breech open, trigger hand reversing and dropping a palm-length cartridge into the breech.

"Jesus, what is that gun, a fifty?"

There followed a brief explanation and comparison of Kulsian versus Earth's "Imperial" caliber nomenclatures. The briefers were two dudes and a tall, spindly woman he had a hard time not staring at.

"So not quite fifty caliber," finished Stabilo, the lead briefing officer, a male SpinDog, and higher muckety-muck. Chalmers didn't like him. First, he was handsome, and second, he said everything with an air of certainty that rubbed Chalmers the wrong way.

On the screen, the bird-thing stumbled, possibly already dead on its feet.

The woman shot again, just to be sure.

\* \* \*

### CLARTHU: MISSION DAY 052

A final shot sounded almost a full minute after the initial flurry, as if the shooter wanted to be sure their target was dead.

Jackson just about bowled Chalmers over trying to get back inside the hetman's home. They'd both thought it was safe to come out, but were jacked up on adrenaline and fear, eyes wide and nuts tight when the shot cracked the quiet. Jackson had only succeeded in shoving the Warrant Officer back toward the entrance before bouncing off Chalmers and onto his ass.

"We good?" Jackson asked, getting back on his feet almost instantly.

Chalmers swallowed and nodded.

When in the shit, Jackson somehow always found cover first. Growing up rough on the South Side of Chicago did that to a kid. Chalmers didn't begrudge it; following his partner's nighpreternatural instincts had saved them both more than once.

The pair blinked a few times in the harsh afternoon light. Unlike most terrestrial towns that had a square, Clarthu was fronted on all but one side by the low buildings the briefings told him were the R'Bak villagers' favored abode. The fourth side, where a place of worship would normally sit, was taken up by the village storehouse.

By the time Chalmers' vision adjusted, Larn was already entering the trench before the door to his neighbor's place, two armed villagers on his heels.

There was some muffled shouting, but no more shots, from inside.

A woman emerged. She had her hands up, a SpinDog manufactured semi-automatic hanging from her forefinger, its slide back to reveal an empty chamber. She offered no resistance as several villagers pulled her from the doorway.

"Damn," Jackson said, hastily holstering his sidearm.

The hetman strode toward them. Chalmers saw a muscle in Larn's jaw jumping as the hetman stared at the woman.

"Shit," Chalmers agreed, recognizing the woman as Kenla, their female guide. Knowing he was a lot slower than Jackson on the draw, he elected to keep his own Beretta out. There were a lot of angry words being exchanged, none of which were spoken by the shooter, who remained serenely aloof in the thicket of angry villagers.

"Where is Ked?" Chalmers said quietly.

Jackson shrugged, eyes on the woman and her captors.

"Orders!" the hetman shouted.

The villagers quieted instantly.

Such discipline impressed Chalmers. In the Mog, a shooting like this would have the whole city rattling off rounds, but the R'Baku didn't seem to have a *khat*-analog, thank God. Then again, rampant stimulant use wasn't the only reason people felt the need to get trigger-happy, not when simple greed with a side of racism and religious fanaticism would do in a pinch.

Chalmers blinked back memories of Somali kids leaving their shot-to-shit homes and only begging for chocolate or digging through UN trash barrels for goodies. When you were a third-generation bullet-dodger used to scavenging for basic necessities, it was easy to miss the big picture, let alone see the root causes of a fucked-up life. Chalmers reminded himself—as he'd had to a few times before—that he was here for a specific mission, not to fix everything.

Beyond the tableau and visions of old memories, he caught sight of a sweating Ked jogging into view from between a couple of buildings.

"What was *he* doing?" Chalmers asked.

"Not his job, that's for sure," Jackson replied.

"You *sure?*"

Jackson's eyes didn't leave Ked. Lips thinning, he shrugged and said, "Fuck. No way to know."

"Right," Chalmers said, eyes sliding back to the hetman.

Larn was in the process of almost reverently disarming the woman.

She said something Chalmers didn't hear.

Larn nodded, said something equally quiet.

Chalmers gestured at Ked, who had either missed or ignored the summons.

"This shit could drive a man to drink," Jackson muttered. "Like get shitfaced-and-falling-outta-my-bunk-drunk."

"You forget the last time we did that?" Chalmers asked, knowing Jackson hadn't.

Chalmers, on the other hand, was quite sure he'd remember that particular bender until the day he died.

\* \* \*

## SPINDOG ROHAB: MISSION DAY 029

A gesture turned off the alarm while Chalmers tried to summon the will to rise from his rack. He'd drunk too much last night. Way too much.

Jackson had needed it. It had started out in good fun: a few drinks, some shit-talking, a few more drinks. Chalmers had been happy to be out from under the fate he'd known awaited him at the end of the helo ride. Jackson had been happy to have survived the crash but was wounded behind the eyes. The liquor had pried the pain out into the open, allowed the small sergeant to begin to express it like the rot at the center of a boil: the two kids and pregnant wife left behind, hundreds of years and more miles away than anyone without a physics degree could even begin to comprehend.

Chalmers glanced across at Jackson, who was snoring, hard, in the next bunk. There at the end, Jackson's anger had boiled over, directionless but still volcanic in its heat.

An unfamiliar guilt washed through Chalmers, made his guts churn even more than the remnants of last night's liquor. Guilty because he, and he alone, should have been the focus of his partner's anger. He could only suppose that Murphy hadn't told the sergeant why, exactly, they'd both been on the helo when they were shot down. Murphy had probably thought telling Jackson would be counter to mission needs or some shit; he might even have been right to withhold the information.

But that didn't make Chalmers feel any better. Indeed, it tested his resolve to *be* better. Should he tell Jackson and blow up the only relationship he'd ever been able to maintain? Just to keep the promise he'd made? Did wanting to be better—*do* better—with this second chance at life give him the right to fuck with Jackson's peace?

Unable to find an answer, Chalmers coughed and, head pounding, sat up. He wouldn't have moved, but two needs drove him: to relieve his bladder and drink something to float his brain, the pan of which was dry-humping every neuron into oblivion. Carefully, oh so carefully, he got up and took care of those needs, then fumbled for the medication the SpinDogs had supplied them with. They said the stuff was harvested on R'Bak, but frankly, Chalmers didn't give a damn. Just so long as it dealt a killing blow to the hangover that threatened to make him hurl.

\* \* \* \* \*

# Chapter Three – Cover

**CLARTHU: MISSION DAY 052**

The crowd started to hurl what sounded like threats at the woman, showing the hetman's control was not as complete as it seemed at first. Kenla was smart enough to remain still, her expression frozen in what Chalmers took to be resignation.

"What should we do, Chalmers?" Jackson asked, head swiveling between Ked and the mob around his sister.

"I don't know," the warrant officer said, certain only that he didn't want to be between the villagers and the target of their anger. He looked again for Ked and saw the warrior shoving his way through the crowd to get to the woman.

Two of the larger villagers pointedly blocked his path. One pushed him. Ked's expression darkened, anger overcoming his initial shock and surprise. The villager ended up flat on his back.

"Shit, we gotta do something, right?"

"Damn it," Chalmers said, watching Ked use a slick move to dump another of the locals on his ass.

"Stop!" Larn barked as several of the villagers turned to deal with the threat charging into their midst.

But Ked was already putting down the next man who laid hands on him; only a few bodies separated him from Larn and Kenla.

Larn wasn't having it, though, and pushed the still-unresisting woman behind him.

Chalmers was moving, but knew he was too late to do anything but witness whatever came next.

Thankfully, Ked hadn't completely lost his senses and tried to get around Larn rather than through him, as he had the other villagers. The older man barely moved, but Ked stumbled away, blood spurting from his nose.

"Cease!" Larn shouted, raising a hand to stop two of his villagers trying to grab Ked. "If you wish to challenge my authority, you must do it properly, Kedlak."

\* \* \*

### SPINDOG ROHAB: MISSION DAY 034

"I'm not challenging your authority, Stabilo, I'm trying to get a proper answer."

"And I am giving you your answer, Chalmers," the SpinDog said, glancing past the "class" toward the hatch at the back of the chamber.

He wanted to call bullshit, but Chalmers wasn't willing to turn his head and see who was there. Murphy, probably, and the warrant officer *really* didn't want another run-in with the major if it could be helped. But a straight answer could mean the difference between life and death, or, more to the major's interest, success or failure.

The initial team—a SEAL, a Vietnam-era Army Special Forces soldier, and Stabilo's own brother, Volo—were already boots on the ground. Chalmers assumed the SEAL had accepted—or been forced to accept, two datapoints Chalmers couldn't take for granted. First, that Volo's life was important enough to the SpinDogs to act as surety of their intent to see the mission through. Second, that Stabilo's family had the full cooperation and endorsement of all SpinDogs. Chalmers knew better. Just because some political boss said everyone was pulling for you, it did not necessarily follow that anyone but the boss was actually pulling for you. Even the boss was suspect until proven otherwise. Especially given the nature of most people's rise to power. And Chalmers had worked under his fair share of shit-climbers.

These data points in mind, he needed to know a lot more about who they would be working with once he and Jackson became the next boots on the ground. "So how do we know we can rely on the locals?"

"Because my family, your hosts, and it being the sole chance of success, assure you of it," the SpinDog said, leveling another quelling look at Chalmers.

Chalmers suppressed a snort. This guy was more arrogant than just about anyone he'd ever met, and he'd been around a lot of arrogant bastards. Almost every single officer he'd ever interrogated as a suspect, for example.

"All right, and why is it *you* are so sure?" Chalmers asked, in his best, "don't bullshit a bullshitter" voice.

If looks could kill, Chalmers would have died right there, been painfully resurrected, and killed a few more times. Stabilo's glare only ended when Murphy cleared his throat. The young SpinDog's gaze flicked up to the older Terran and back to his tormentor.

Chalmers couldn't help but smile beatifically.

"Rest assured, the people of Clarthu will be amenable to contact," Stabilo tried again.

Chalmers shook his head and looked to Murphy.

"Warrant Officer Chalmers has a need to know, Stabilo."

"Very good, Major Murphy." Chalmers didn't miss the way Stabilo's lip started to curl before the younger man got control. "We've been in contact with the villagers for generations. They provide us information and certain biologicals we cannot easily obtain elsewhere; we provide them with certain technological items they cannot make themselves."

"Like what? How much? How often?"

"I am afraid I cannot answer those questions with specificity."

Chalmers shook his head again, hoping the major would jump in and stomp the local into a more cooperative mood.

But Murphy, rather than piling the pressure on, asked, "Maybe if you explain exactly what you want, Chalmers?"

Chalmers answered Murphy directly, ignoring a fuming Stabilo, "I need to know what these people value so I can either predict which way they'll jump if someone offers them a deal to sell us out or where to apply pressure if I have to question one of them regarding a crime they commit."

"Question?" Stabilo's smile was a razor. "I think you overestimate how civilized these people are. There is no…'rule of law,' I think you call it?"

Chalmers nodded.

A wider, predatory smile from Stabilo. "No, none of that. Like as not, if accused of some crime, the average R'Bak nomad will insist on trial by combat."

"And the villagers, the city-dwellers?" Chalmers asked.

"Most will have ground staked out for such, and formal judges to rule in those cases where both parties die as a result of the trial by combat."

\* \* \*

## CLARTHU: MISSION DAY 052

"Trial by combat! I demand trial by combat!" the woman shouted in answer to something Larn said to Ked, who was still prone on the ground. "Who will stand in the circle?"

"I, Kenla Aksinos, will stand for myself in this. Your son raped me. I avenged myself upon him. I am innocent of wrongdoing under the laws of both the Kedlak and the Clarth."

The hetman raised his voice as well, arms lifted to silence the gathered people. "I dispute your right to vengeance, as you provided no proof to the people of his wrongdoing. As my son's widows are both with child, they cannot stand in the circle. Therefore, I will face you myself."

"Shit," Jackson muttered. "Does that mean—"

"She killed his son?" Chalmers said, finishing the thought.

The villagers shouted bloodthirsty encouragement to their leader, and the mass of them started toward the staked grounds at the far end of the village.

Ked, forgotten in the drama, climbed to his feet and edged through the crowd to join Chalmers and Jackson. His expression was guarded but calmer than that of either of the off-worlders.

"What the hell, Ked?"

The indig nodded toward the last of the locals as they departed, bringing one finger to his lips to ask for silence.

Chalmers and Jackson waited impatiently for the last of the villagers to leave the small square before the hetman's dwelling.

"You wanted to check the homes, no? Look for radio of collaborator who communicates with the City?"

"What?" Jackson asked.

"You mean you arranged all that?" Chalmers asked.

The indig's shrug was eloquent. "My sister wish revenge." He gestured at the hetman's residence. "She will make the fight last as long as she can, but we waste time."

Jackson's eyes were a bit wild. "She's not likely to survive, is she?"

Ked shrugged again, and the bone charms decorating his bandoliers clicked as he moved to the hetman's door. "Honor demanded this action."

Chalmers hurried after. "But not of *you*?" he asked, hearing Jackson follow.

Ked's surprised glance told Chalmers he'd put a foot in it. "Of course not. Kenla was attacked by Lornsos. As she is not with child as a result, she avenged herself, removing the stain to her honor."

Chalmers shook his head. "But the trial?"

He shrugged. "She is better at blades than I." He bent and led the way into the hetman's home.

The Lost Soldiers followed. The central room was as they'd left it: quiet, comfortable, and spartan. Ked quickly crossed to the curtained alcove at the back where the hetman slept, presumably.

"What size thing do we search for?"

"A very small chest. Might have a crank on it." This much, at least, he'd accepted from the SpinDog briefer: while the Kulsians had some machinery that was far more advanced than what he was used to, they were not likely to give any high-end technology to the indig collaborators this far from centers of power. The rig was supposed to look something like a transistor radio, with a hand crank similar to those on AM/FM survival sets from Chalmers' own era.

Ked rummaged around in the alcove while Chalmers searched the main chamber and Jackson watched the entrance.

It didn't take more than two minutes to search. The villagers were maybe one step up from nomads themselves, and even the hetman's possessions offered very little in the way of hiding places.

"Nothing?"

Ked shook his head. "Nothing."

\* \* \* \* \*

# Chapter Four – Outmaneuvered

"**N**othing," Chalmers said automatically, feeling as if he'd been caught with one hand in the cookie jar. "Nothing useful," he amended, slowly returning his hands to the oddly-designed SpinDog keyboard.

Jackson snorted. "Man, you have a shit startle response." The sergeant looked better than he had before they'd gone into the virtual reality language training. Time, it seemed, even virtual time spent slogging through the odd complexities of devolved Ktoran grammar and syntax, healed many things. "In fact," Jackson continued after a dramatic pause, "you may have the worst startle response of anyone I've ever worked with. Totally useless."

"Might be, Jacks, might be." Chalmers rubbed his chin and the five o'clock shadow there. "But it's only a result of my need to protect my pretty face."

"Keep telling yourself that, man," Jackson said, casting a meaningful look at Chalmers' display.

"I was looking at the history files," Chalmers said carefully. They'd been cooling their heels since the SEAL's mission had launched, spending a lot of time in a seemingly-endless string of briefings and planning sessions. Despite all the meetings, Murphy was being cagey about when, exactly, their deployment would happen. Tonight had been their first time off in a while, and Chalmers

45

had decided to turn over a new leaf and started researching their allies. What he'd found hadn't satisfied him, not at all. He'd looked for more juicy material, something equivalent to a gossip rag or tell-all book, but the SpinDogs either didn't have such things or were keeping the Lost Soldiers locked out of the public information stream.

"Not much there," Jackson said. "Makes you think they got shit to hide."

Chalmers nodded at the computer screen. "Maybe we can hack it, you know, like *War Games*? You get much time on computers as a kid?" he asked, hoping against hope the younger man would have some hidden skill at computers he hadn't known about.

"'Course, man!" Jackson chuckled. "Growing up on the South Side in the early eighties got us kids all sorts of time on them main-frames. In fact, I was gonna go straight to work for IBM right up until I signed my first contract with the Bulls."

Chalmers was laughing well before Jackson finished his sarcastic rant. He held his hands up in surrender. "All right, all right! I'm an asshole."

"No, you just showing your vanilla," Jackson said, smiling.

"All right, I deserved that..." He gestured at the terminal as well. "But you've been reading up, right?"

"Damn straight."

"The files they gave us; they're pretty scant on who hates who."

Jackson shrugged narrow shoulders. "Well, kinda understandable."

Chalmers looked a question at him.

"They're making a mistake like the one mistake *you* just made. Only on a lot bigger scale."

"Not sure I follow," Chalmers said.

"The SpinDogs all seem to think their way is *the* way, so why bother learning what others think or do?"

Chalmers shook his head slightly. "Yeah, but these guys are supposed to be all, 'survival of the fittest' and warrior culture. Seems like holding back basic information would create issues of survival for anyone who was that blind, and those acting on that blindness."

"Crackers gonna be crackers." Jackson delivered the words with a southern drawl that he seemed to think should underline his meaning.

Underlining or no, Chalmers missed what he meant. "What?" he asked.

"Look at their history—at least what we've been told of it. They were bound to think of themselves as the best and brightest thing going, and their arrogant asses won't let them admit that losing their own civil war—or whatever—was their own damn fault. So, they get kicked out of the house and come here, finding all these backward people, a lot of who've descended into some kind of worse-than-Thunderdome shit. They all set to claim themselves the new masters, but then the Kulsians appear, who haven't descended quite so far, and they got big guns, too, and better numbers. But our friends were lucky enough to be in space, so they hide out, bide their time, all the while thinking their truth is the only truth that matters. When really, what's goin' on is one cracker sees the other cracker got a bigger whip and knows, deep in his bones, that he wants to hold that whip, but can't."

"You lost me again, Jackson," Chalmers said.

Jackson sighed, thought about it a moment, then said, "These SpinDogs have had nothing smack them in the face to tell them how wrong their outlook is."

"But they were kicked off their home world or whatever."

Jackson nodded emphatically. "Sure were. But to their minds, they got beat by people who were *better* than they were at being the ideal of their culture. They come here, see the people that lost some of the motherland's stink, all descended into barbarism, and the folks that didn't sink *as* low still in charge, still adhering to the Old Ways. Nothing has ever told these crackers their system is whacked. They don't even think to question that. The only lesson they've learned is the wrong one: that *they* weren't good *enough* at working that system, which only served to *confirm*, in their eyes, the values of the very same system, man."

Chalmers blinked. He'd always known Jackson was smarter than he, but he'd rarely been shown just how *much* smarter. If the man had been given a better education, Chalmers had no doubt Jackson would have been some kind of staff officer or civilian bigwig.

Guilt followed the thought. Guilt that, had Jackson not fallen in with the wrong crowd, so many things might have been different. Especially since, in this case, the wrong crowd was one Horace Chalmers, Warrant Officer, US Army.

"Yeah," Jackson mused, staring at the bulkhead, "Murphy seems to think things are going to be fine once we put our hosts in charge of the planet. Maybe it's just my blood talking, but I'm thinking we just putting *our* crackers in charge, nothing more."

"Is that a problem?"

Another pensive shrug. "Not really. I figure the government used to do the same shit all the time, right? So long as we know what our crackers want, we can be looking out, I guess…No, thing I worry about is this: do we really know our crackers, or are they gonna be stabbing each other—and us—in the back to get the best bits of the pig?"

Chalmers leaned back, suddenly wishing they hadn't had this conversation in what passed for public. Not that there were any sureties of privacy elsewhere, but if Jackson was right, Chalmers was certain all of the competing interests would act to make sure their agenda was served. And that could interfere with the mission. Almost certainly would, in fact.

He didn't think he was being paranoid, but just because you couldn't see threats didn't mean they weren't there. That's why he'd been diligently searching through the records they'd been given. Wanting to name his fear made Chalmers a far better student than he'd been before.

Come to think of it, the emphasis all the non-Terran humans— SpinDogs, R'Bak, and Kulsians alike—placed on clan loyalty was a lot like Mogadishu, what with its powerful warlords and would-be kings.

No, this could end up *being* the Mog all over again, no matter who they wound up backing in the end.

* * *

### CLARTHU: MISSION DAY 052

In the end, searching several additional houses didn't produce the radio; Chalmers stalked out of the third, still empty-handed. Time constraints had been such that, after the hetman's home, they had to split up to cover more ground, but even working one to a structure, Ked, Jackson, and he were not going to get much accomplished. Even if they'd had a Gestapo-like disregard for the personal property of their allies, tossing a place was no substitute for a careful, thorough search.

They needed time they simply were not going to have, not if the noises rising from the dueling ground were the bad sign they seemed to be. The ritualized, chant-like shouts had become more frenzied since the three had split up. Any long fight was a hard fight, Chalmers knew.

"Chalmers!" Ked said, emerging from the large building across from the hetman's home.

The crowd noise changed again, became a series of rousing cheers as Chalmers jogged over.

"Is this it?" Ked asked. He held what looked like a metal-framed bread-box with a dynamo crank protruding from one end.

Chalmers smiled at the younger man. "Sure is! Where was it?"

"Inside. Village grain store. Buried about arm-length."

Chalmers cursed. Right where it would make it impossible to single someone out as the owner, so long as you didn't leave fingerprints. For perhaps the third time since wakening in these strange circumstances, Chalmers lamented the fact he had no evidence kit with him.

Another cheer rose from the dueling ground. Chalmers glanced at Ked, wondering how the man could be so cool while his sister was fighting for her life a few hundred yards away.

"Jackson, come on, man," Chalmers called as loudly as he darted into the doorway of the home belonging to the hetman's son.

"I'm coming, Chalmers," Jackson grunted. "Hold your shit."

"Ked found the radio, man."

"Right," Jackson said, walking backward out of the building. Chalmers could hear him dragging something.

"What the shit, Jacks?" Chalmers asked as he saw the trunk his partner was dragging. Except, on second glance, it wasn't a trunk at all. Covered in whinnie-hide, the thing looked like a treasure chest out of one of his old D&D books, five feet long by three feet high.

"Check this shit out," Jackson said, flipping the lid up.

Chalmers whistled. "That ain't right." And it wasn't.

Nestled within the chest was a shipping crate full of what looked like anti-tank missiles. Five of them and the single-tube device that, judging from a button-studded box which extruded from one part, had to be the launcher.

"Shit, man, those had to come from—"

Another cheer, this one louder than those previous, erupted from the grounds. It was cut short by a collective gasp that left a silence as troubling as anything that had come before.

"Thinking we should put it back, no?" Chalmers said, wondering what the villagers would make of them looting a dead man's possessions.

"I don't think so. I figure we give the hetman a look at what his son was up to," Jackson said, patting the lid.

"And if they bought them?" Chalmers asked, looking hopefully at Ked.

The warrior scratched at his sparse beard thoughtfully but ultimately shook his head. "Nothing the villagers have in trade is worth so much as these."

"And then there is the why. These are not so useful against men, but against machines," Jackson mused.

"But the J'Stull don't come out to these parts—"

"Not according to our friend Stabilo, anyway," Chalmers said.

The crowd noise had receded to a lower, steady volume.

Ked sighed, the set of his shoulders easing.

"What is it, Ked?"

"My sister is victorious," he said, pushing the radio into Chalmers' hands.

Chalmers blinked. "How do you know?"

"They do not cheer for her as they would for their hetman. I go to see if she needs healing. I will return."

"Wait! Should we put this back?" Chalmers asked, gesturing toward the chest.

A shrug. "I do not know. The hetman may be dead. We will find out in a few moments. His son is already dead, and so beyond caring if caught with it."

Chalmers stared after Kedlak. "Jacks," he mumbled, "we are standing in broad-daylight holding two pieces of evidence that prove some local is a traitor."

"Yeah," the sergeant agreed sourly, "which means we the only ones holding the bag that someone's ready to kill over."

Chalmers spat. The mission just kept getting better and better.

\* \* \*

### SPINDOG ROHAB: MISSION DAY 048

"Man, this mission just keeps getting better and better," Jackson said, replacing the headset on the terminal.

"What's that?" Chalmers asked, mopping a sweaty brow with one end of his towel. The .75-gee maintained in the quarters of most SpinDog habs wasn't enough to maintain real muscle tone, not on its own, so the afternoon workout he had just returned from had quickly become a habit. His body had likely been in the best shape it had been since AIT on his awakening, and it was easier to start from that high level of fitness than it had been at any time since his youth. He needed *something* to be easier, too. This changing his life for the better the second time around wasn't exactly easy, so he figured making a habit of healthy practices was better than trying to play catch up later.

"You see the latest mission brief?" Jackson asked, leaning back in his chair to avoid getting sweat dripped on him. The Coriolis effect made it hard to predict just where shit was gonna hit.

"No. What happened?" Chalmers asked, his gut suddenly churning.

"Murphy said we're no longer going to be tasked with locating black market dealers and their suppliers, but uncovering spies in the local populace."

Nodding, Chalmers finished wiping down and, wadding the towel in one fist, chucked it into the reclaimer built into the wall of their quarters.

"You don't seem surprised."

Chalmers shrugged and skinned off his sweat-soaked shirt. "Nope. Murphy doesn't know any better than us what we're gonna see on the ground until...well, until we're boots on the ground. I figure we could end up doing anything from carrying beans and bullets for the shooters to driving one of those goofy armored vehicles the local warlords tool around in. There's just no way of knowing until we are down and doing it. Murphy's Law screws with even the simplest plans, and this one has way too many ifs for comfortable planning."

"How are you so chill, man? No offense, but your ass wasn't exactly known for coolness..."

Chalmers smiled. "I figure I got a second chance at doing this right. Being...better, I guess? Life being life, that don't mean the chance doesn't have a heavy price tag attached, but I'd rather get it right, you know? For me."

Jackson smiled. "You got all wise and shit, Chalmers."

"I'm trying, Jacks. I'm trying."

\* \* \* \* \*

# Chapter Five –
# Cut Me a Slice

### CLARTHU: MISSION DAY 052

"I'm trying to *something* from your point of view, but I just can't seem to give a *something* begroag shit, Ked," Kenla said, a toss of her head making several of the tiny bones in her dreadlocks click against one another. Kenla's right arm was in a sling and there was a bandage around her midriff, but the bandage showed surprisingly little blood, especially since the trousers she wore still glistened with the stuff down to her knees. A third wrapping covered the place where her neck joined her shoulder.

"You overcame and survived, did you not?" Ked asked, sounding defensive and, from the flushed reddening of his ears, knowing it.

"No thanks to your medicine! I had to be treated by the village healer, here," she gestured with her unbound arm at one of the women walking behind her. The hetman was being carried into his home, and the healer's progress was slowed by the bearers and their charge as they negotiated the entrance. "They showed honor, though, treating me before their own."

"Is he alive?" Chalmers asked.

More clicking of bones followed as she shrugged. "He was when he fell at my feet, though just barely. I cut him many times, but he is tough as old leather," Kenla opined.

*Deadlier than the male.* The quote crossed his mind before Chalmers could remember where he'd heard it.

"He will live," the village healer said. "I have given him the *patheos-pak*, and his natural endurance will replenish his blood within a day or two."

"The what?" Chalmers asked, but the healer ducked into the entrance, and Ked and his sister had their heads together, speaking quietly.

Amazingly, the rest of the villagers seemed uninterested in the chest Jackson had dragged from the dead man's home. Chalmers had been watching. No one seemed to take any undue notice or care.

He'd hid the radio in his pack, so there remained three possibilities: one, the collaborator responsible for the transmissions was smooth enough to avoid gawking; two, the collaborator who had the radio had not been responsible for the weapons as well; or three, the collaborator and man killed by Kenla were one and the same.

"You see anything?" the warrant officer asked Jackson, in English.

"No. You?"

Chalmers shook his head. He considered a moment, then added, "We'll have to watch tonight, then. I can't see this going unreported to whoever provided those missiles."

Jackson nodded. When the siblings had finished their quiet conference, he repeated the plan in the local dialect. The more of it they heard and spoke, the more they realized it had a lot less Ktoran in it than what the SpinDogs spoke.

Kenla considered the instructions. "It will not be easy to watch unobserved, War Technician Chalmers."

"I will do it," her brother said.

Chalmers did not miss the glance she leveled at her brother. Wondering what it meant, he decided to keep an eye on both of them as well as the grain store tonight. He would, as Ronnie RayGun had said, "Trust but confirm."

\* \* \*

### SPINDOG SHUTTLE: MISSION DAY 051

"Trust but confirm. Trust but confirm. Trust but confirm," Chalmers grunted the litany into his helmet.

"What?" Jackson gasped.

Chalmers didn't answer right away, fighting for breath after saying so much.

Their shuttle had been burning for what the SpinDogs termed, "a narrow drop window to orbital insertion." This "Spaceman Spiff" speech translated roughly as, "An absurdly fidgety three-hundred-pound trucker will be sitting on your chest, gut, and bladder for at least thirty minutes, have a nice day." The Dornaani ship on which they'd arrived in-system compared to their current ride much like a Ferrari compared to a Mustang, both were powerful and looked pretty, depending on taste, but one certainly seemed a lot more refined than the other. Even so, the shuttle *looked* more advanced than anything Earth had been sending into orbit and was certainly powerful enough to push his eyeballs through the back of his skull.

He'd just decided that concentrating on speaking would at least take his mind off the struggle that simply breathing had become when the thrust suddenly cut back to something like one gee.

Chalmers breathed in and out, repeating the process twice, just to be sure his ribs were in their proper place, before he finally replied, "I was just wishing we could have confirmed this thing was safe before being packed in like sardines."

Jackson pulled a face, his expression clearly visible through the visor of his space suit's helmet.

"What was that, Space Man?" Chalmers asked, more than a little freaked out by the fact that he was in a fucking space suit, too.

"I fucking *hate* sardines."

Chalmers laughed. "I'm sure they love you."

"Naw, man. My pops, he used to make us get them on our pizza."

"On pizza?"

"Yes."

"You sure you're talking about sardines? I heard of anchovies on pizza, but not sardines."

Jackson's eyes were a little wild. "I'm talkin' sardines. You know: those fish in oil. Stink to high heaven."

"Both are packed in oil. Anchovies are smaller, I think."

"Sardine, anchovies, whatever, man," Jackson said, calmer for having something other than their predicament to talk about. "They used to stink like nothing else. Would make the whole house smell, even when he only got half the pizza covered with that crap."

"That's…unnatural," Chalmers said, meaning it. "In fact, it should be against the Geneva Conventions."

"I *know!*" Jackson sniffed, shook his head. "Miss that guy. Not the pizzas, though. Not those fish-smelling, nasty-ass pizzas!"

"Pizza," Chalmers said, reminded of the best he'd ever had. "Knew this place in SF made a killer slice: pineapple and ham."

"Fruit? You put *fruit* on your pizza? Talk about violating the Conventions, man. That's just wrong, man. Just *wrong*. At least fish is meat."

"Fish ain't meat, man."

"The fuck it ain't. Who the hell asks the asshole who thinks putting fruit on a piece of pie is a good idea, anyway? No one, that's who!"

"For God sakesss—" Chalmers' retort was pressed out of him in a distorted *hiss* as the pilot piled on the gees again.

\* \* \*

### CLARTHU: MISSION DAY 052

The hissing and grunting resumed.

"For God's sakes!" Chalmers muttered, kicking the grunting little alien lizard-goat off his foot for the tenth time.

The goat—well, *begroag*—was a tiny, more stupid, and, if this one was a good example, more inbred cousin to the whinnies that the locals used as pack animals. Normally this would not have impacted Chalmers one bit. Normally.

But Murphy's Law was in effect, and this begroag had decided Chalmers' boot was a fine source of food or sex; Chalmers wasn't sure which. Both, maybe? Every few minutes Chalmers was forced to kick it away, and it would get the hint for a little while before coming back at odd intervals to bite, then hump and shimmy against his foot. He was leaning toward the idea it wanted to make babies, simply because it was so utterly persistent. Nothing was that hungry. Horny, yes. Hungry...nah.

It was obvious the creatures had been domesticated for the same reasons humans—well, *Terrans*—kept goats, for food and keeping the weeds down, so it was definitely someone's property. Which made it out of bounds for a more permanent solution than a boot to the head. He could think of no better way to piss off a farmer or herder than killing their livestock, so shooting the damn thing off his boot was not an option, even if he could do it silently.

The stakeout was one of the least onerous he'd ever been on. Unadjusted to R'Bak's shorter days, he'd found it easy to stay awake well into the nine-hour night, even without the constant attempted boot-buggery of the begroag and despite the warm earthen berm he was stretched out and hiding on.

Jackson was on the far side of the village, watching the eastern approaches to the grain store. Ked was supposed to be watching the western side of the village, and Chalmers was watching him from what he hoped was a concealed position. Something had been off in the man's responses after the duel, and Chalmers didn't trust him. Kenla was still in the healer's hut, recovering from blood loss, though she seemed awfully chipper for someone who'd been cut so many times. Chalmers had no doubt these people were hard. It remained to be seen if they were trustworthy.

Shaking clear of other concerns, Chalmers focused all his attention on what he could do. A moment later he was grateful he'd decided to pay closer attention. He wasn't sure what it was, but something was different. Movement? He peered into the twilight, but couldn't pick out exactly what had triggered the feeling.

He slowed his breathing, straining to hear.

A maddening itch started just above the top of his left boot, distracting him. He reached down to address the issue and found something wet, warm, and sticky left behind by the begroag. He brought his hand up and stared at glistening fingers in the dimness. Fighting the urge to shriek in horror, leap to his feet, fetch the nearest flamethrower, and *burn* his fingers, leg, and boots clean off, he caught movement out of the corner of his eye.

Overcoming the urge to incinerate, Chalmers again tried to concentrate on the sound heard just moments before.

Among the shadows and blank darkness where Ked had hidden, there was a flicker of movement, then another, then Ked's slim figure emerged into the dim light of R'Bak's distant secondary star. He crouched, peering intently toward the storehouse.

Scrubbing his begroag-scummed hand on the rough soil of the berm, Chalmers slowly, and as quietly as he could, raised himself from the ground. As the begroag started to amble closer for another go, he set out toward the building more quickly than quietly, not wanting another sliming.

Ked, meanwhile, had moved from one shadow to the next, and was nearly at the door to the storehouse. The indig disappeared into shadow again before briefly reappearing alongside the black rectangle that marked the storehouse's recessed entryway.

Chalmers could see another figure—Jackson—closing on the same spot.

A muffled cry and then a thump sounded from inside as the partners arrived within a few steps of each other.

Jackson drew his sidearm and glanced at Chalmers, who had decided to remain empty-handed in case he had to go hands-on.

\* \* \* \* \*

# Chapter Six –
# Apologies Forthcoming

"**H**ands-on experience is essential, Jackson," Chalmers said, glad the brush fire burning almost ten miles to the south wasn't likely to be along their path. Of course, any of the more naturally occurring ones might become a problem.

Wishing to limit their exposure to hostile eyes, the big, snub-nosed shuttle had landed in as sparsely settled an area as possible. The main mission, of course, meant they were still fairly close to one of the satrapies, as those states were the ones that protected Kulsian interests in their overlord's absence. An anxious-looking SpinDog crew had thrown the two Lost Soldiers and their equipment out as soon as the vehicles from Camp Stark appeared on the horizon. Then, quite literally in this case, they burned for orbit. The massive rocket engines of the shuttle had ignited the grass fire that still smoldered in the distance.

"'Hands-on experience is necessary?' You tryin' to sell me that? Really?" Jackson asked, his expression making it all too clear he knew Chalmers was full of shit. Chalmers sensed his partner was arguing as much to distract them both from the oddly astringent brush smoke being carried on the pre-dawn wind as any strong desire to drive the buggy for himself.

"Look, dude, I drove these things all over Baja." It was an exaggeration, of course. He couldn't be sure, but Chalmers was reasonably confident he'd driven one for an hour or two one drunken week in Mexico. He'd done a *lot* of drinking on that vacation, as he'd been celebrating—or trying to forget—the demise of his second marriage. Come to think of it, he just might have spent more than a couple hours behind the wheel.

He shook his head, unable to recall. There had been *lots* of mescal.

"Fine," Jackson grunted.

Chalmers knew he wasn't living up to the promise he'd made to be a better man and not lie about things, but damn it, he *really* wanted to drive the buggy.

The all-wheel weirdness was every kind of post-apocalyptic *Mad Max* cool: seating for four with a steel tube chassis riding high on beefy shocks. The buggy made his hands itch with desire to drive it.

He bent to examine the tires, which proved to be perfectly tailored to the sand, dust, and loose, stony soil composition of the terrain. They were even partially deflated to provide the best possible purchase and a spare was mounted on each side behind a rank of jerry cans.

And the cool didn't end there. The large, exposed engine had made a satisfying growl when it was driven up to them by a gearhead from Camp Stark's new motor pool. The grease monkey might have been ex-army, but just whose army it had been was hard to say; he'd had Cyrillic tattoos across his fingers. He also looked resentful at having to part with the stolen machine as he climbed into the truck that had accompanied him out into the god-forsaken wastes and was now carrying him back to the forward operating base. Might have just been jealousy over the fact the two new arrivals were being given *any* kind of vehicle to complete their mission, but Chalmers doubted it. Neither fuel nor spares were easily come by, and their operation was being carefully controlled to avoid waste. Once the Lost Soldiers ran out of those logistical necessities, the vehicles liberated from the Kulsian cache would go from being indispensable to oversized paperweights.

"You acting like this thing is a saddle-whinnie, Chalmers," Jackson said as he removed his pack and settled it behind the rear passenger seat. The cargo area was small, and he had to move the strap of a come-along to get it in place.

"Am not," Chalmers said. "Though I would pay money to see you try to ride, city boy."

"Look at you, talking shit like you some kinda John Wayne or something."

"Naw, just a part-time redneck. We like gears and engines more than steers and horses and shit."

"That why you rednecks have all them broke-down cars and refrigerators and shit on your front lawns?" Jackson asked as he loosened another come-along strap to make room so Chalmers could drop his pack next to Jackson's own.

Chalmers chuckled. "Must be."

The combined communications and GPS—or whatever—unit attached to Jackson's pack pinged.

Jackson glanced at Chalmers, who nodded. The sergeant unclipped the carabiner securing the device to his bag and held it up. A touch of his thumb activated it.

"Gentlemen." Murphy's voice was clear and cool, like the predawn air. "Are you ready?"

"As much as we can be, not knowing where we're headed," Chalmers said, keeping his tone as light and non-confrontational as he could, even as he wished for video so he could read Murphy's expression.

"Sorry about that. OpSec has to be very tight on this one." The major made a point of pausing.

Jackson and Chalmers both perked up at this, making a check of their surroundings. No one was close enough to listen in without being obvious about it or using vanishingly rare electronics.

"You're to meet with a couple of the kinsmen from the Sarmatchani tribes. They're from the next tribe over and have more contact with the settled peoples we are eventually going to have to get on our side. The tribesmen will help you make contact with the people of Clarthu."

The device in Jackson's hand lit up with a map and coordinates.

"Orbital SIGINT intercepted a radio transmission during our last movement near Clarthu. The same guys decoded the message, and it was a fairly accurate report of our movements and numbers during and since we seized the Kulsian vehicles and equipment."

"Shit," Jackson muttered.

"The indig tribesmen we've been dealing with say the villagers are predisposed to support us, too, which tracks generally with the HUMINT the SpinDogs have been sharing with us. Therefore, both intelligence streams believe it's one, or possibly two, collaborators."

"But how much can we trust the SpinDogs?" Chalmers asked.

Murphy paused again, clearly aware their hosts would know exactly what he was saying over their own comm system. "While the SpinDogs have been…less than entirely forthcoming on certain matters, they have fully supported the mission. I think this particular situation might have something to do with the RockHounds faction or the friction between the Expansionists and the Hardliners. Frankly, I don't know."

"The who?" Chalmers asked.

"Internal political blocs," Murphy answered. "Well, the last two are entirely internal matters, the other not so much…" He trailed off.

Chalmers and Jackson both waited, knowing any information the major had was likely to be important background.

When he resumed speaking, it was clear Murphy was choosing his words with even more care. "The Expansionists are the political bloc of SpinDogs who want to take over here and are therefore, at least partially, responsible for supporting us. The Hardliners traditionally resist change and are opposed to almost all of the Expansionsts' strategies and proposals. The RockHounds are an entirely separate group from the SpinDogs. They are essentially miners and prospectors who spend most of their lives in deep space. They have their own internal political fault lines, of which I am mostly ignorant." Again, a thoughtful pause. "There's a lot of complexity, and we've only begun to scratch the surface."

"Poles," Chalmers said, equally thoughtfully.

"What's that, Chief?" Murphy asked.

"Just thinking we have to be wary of being used up like the Polish Paras in WWII," Chalmers explained.

Murphy was silent for a long moment, then said, "There are some parallels, but I hope to keep everyone from dying because we over-extended and reached for a bridge too far. Or further."

Chalmers smiled weakly. Murphy still intimidated the shit out of him, but it was good to hear the major recognize the quality of his assessment.

"At any rate, gentlemen, I need you to collect your tribal guides, obtain their best assessment of who might be radioing in our dispositions and why. With that information in hand—or not—you will then proceed to the village where you will locate and confiscate any radio equipment before our next movement. You will accomplish all of this while minimizing any damage to our future relations with the villagers as potential future allies. I am told that Bruce—er, Lieutenant Lee—is done with her shakedown flights and will be standing off for emergency extraction during the meet with the Kedlak."

"You suspect Kedlak's people will give us trouble?" Chalmers asked, relieved there was some kind of plan to get them out if things dropped in the shitter.

"No, but I know I wouldn't want to meet with a tribe of unknowns without some kind of extraction team, and I won't send people to do things I wouldn't do myself." The major paused. "And before you ask, I considered having her loiter above the meet, but we don't know precisely where the camp is, and I don't want to spook them."

"Spook them?" Chalmers asked.

Jackson shot a look at Chalmers the latter interpreted as, "Why don't you pay attention to the briefings?"

Murphy, unaware of the silent byplay and apparently willing to overlook Chalmers' ignorance, said, "The only people with air power on R'Bak are the bad guys, and we don't want our first impression to be tainted by that association." Murphy then added, "Look, I know this mission's a dog's breakfast, but I need you to execute, copy?"

"Copy that," Jackson said.

"Any questions?"

"What kind of toast you want with that order?" Jackson asked.

"Blackened rye," Murphy drawled.

"And how long do we have to accomplish the mission?" Chalmers asked, glad the major was cozy with one of them, at least.

"Oh, I'm sure two crack investigators like you can sew this up in forty-eight hours. In forty-nine and one-half hours the lead elements of our force will be transiting the valley in full view of the village. Gentlemen, I would really hate to level a village because of one asshole. Find the radio. Find the operator. I'm not too concerned about the condition of either, but stopping the transmissions is priority one. Hooah?"

"Hooah, Major," the partners chorused, even though neither of them were, or had been, Rangers. The query-and-response had been ubiquitous among the Airborne guys in Mogadishu, and some things spread—and stuck in the head—like herpes.

The link went dead.

"I'm still driving," Chalmers said, rushing around to the driver's side of the buggy.

Jackson let Chalmers go, ratcheting the come-along until their packs were held firmly in place.

Chalmers hopped in and started the little rear-engined vehicle, which came snorting to life.

Startled by the sudden, angry growl from so close at hand, Jackson banged his head against a roll bar and spat a string of invective at Chalmers in multiple languages.

"Sorry, man."

\* \* \*

## CLARTHU: MISSION DAY 052

"Sorry, man," Jackson said.

"Fuck you," Chalmers grunted, rubbing his back just above the kidney, knowing he'd have a muzzle-shaped bruise there in the morning.

Chalmers had stumbled over a prone Ked as he entered the storehouse. Jackson, following too closely, had inadvertently jammed the muzzle of his .45 into his partner's back.

Reaching blindly with his left hand for a pulse at Ked's throat, Chalmers drew his own pistol with his right. Trying to do too many things at once, he failed at all of them. Forcing himself to slow down, he found Ked's neck and the carotid. A strong pulse pushed against his fingers.

"Lights," Chalmers hissed, fumbling with his left hand for the newly manufactured Vietnam-era, L-angle, red-lens flashlight they'd been issued for the mission. He slid the switch to on. If the other Lost Soldiers were as troubled as Chalmers was over using a device manufactured on a fucking asteroid some hundred and more years after the original design was considered completely outdated, they hadn't shown it. Then again, Li-ion batteries and LEDs were not always better than alkaline and incandescents and second chances didn't always result in improvement. It was another sign that, regardless of whether it was a second chance, it was fucking weird, this life. Then again, the same could be said for Army life, though there had been more people to look at and shrug in silent commiseration back in the Green Machine.

Immune to his thoughts, red light illuminated the short hall to the storeroom. Unlike Clarthu's homes, the storehouse didn't have a doglegged entrance. Rather, the hallway was broad, probably to facilitate transportation of the harvest in and out of the place. One of the two rough-hewn wood doors at the end of the passage was ajar, a few inches of blackness showing in the opening.

"Cover," Chalmers said.

"Covering." Jackson modified his stance, the pistol steadied with the hand holding the flashlight. He'd been to the range with some of the Vietnam-era boys, it seemed.

Chalmers looked down. Ked's head was damp, slick with blood that looked black under the red light. There wasn't a pool under his cheek, so he wasn't bleeding that much.

"No one got past you, did they?" Chalmers whispered.

Jackson shook his head.

"All right. Let's clear it."

"Copy."

The pair advanced on the doors, each to one side of the hallway, Chalmers on the side with the door ajar.

Ked started snoring, the sudden noise shattering the quiet and nearly startling Chalmers into pulling the trigger. He shook his head and, grinding his teeth in frustration, watched the doors as they advanced.

The doors opened toward them and Chalmers nodded at them as they drew close enough to pull the big wooden handles. Sweat began to prickle his hairline.

Jackson reached across and pushed the one in front of Chalmers all the way open with his flashlight.

Gun up, Chalmers rolled in as swiftly and smoothly as he could. A long, empty aisle stretched about twenty yards, ending on a wall. Every third yard an opening yawned on either side of the aisle, each providing access to a bin-like holding area, fronted by a knee-high pony wall.

Jackson entered and went to the other side, pistol and flashlight up and at the ready.

Sweat began to roll off Chalmers' brow and threaten his vision as he sliced the pie to take a look inside the first chamber opposite.

There were great big—he did a double-take; no, Indiana Jones-sized—baskets stacked two high across the width of the chamber, tight fitting lids in place to defy any monkey that might give away their quarry. He was tempted to shake his head to get rid of the movie image. "Hope this guy brought a sword to a gunfight, too," Chalmers muttered.

Jackson's stifled "What the fuc—?" was interrupted as a figure trailing a fog of grain dust burst from the opening he was covering and ran straight at him.

The sergeant's .45 didn't *bang*, it BOOMED, straining Chalmers' already-frayed nerves to the breaking point and just beyond. The warrant officer, never a steely-eyed gunfighter, yelped and flinched, yanking the trigger on his own Beretta. It BOOMED, too. Missing both Jackson and the person rushing him, the fat lead round *spanged* off the bricks beside Jackson and ricocheted down the corridor with an evil *wheet-wheet* sound that made Chalmers' sack draw up.

Meanwhile, the silhouette rushing Jackson folded and fell into him, wheezing wetly.

"God damn!" Jackson yelled, shoving the wounded figure back, hard, with the muzzle of his still-smoking gun. The person toppled over onto their back.

Ignoring the persistent *EEeeeeee* in his ears, Chalmers steadied his flashlight on the target, saw it was a woman and blinked, wondering where he knew her from.

"The medic or whatever," Jackson said, the .45 in his hand rattling loudly as he lowered it. The after-effects of adrenaline were making the weapon—an exact copy of the Vietnam-era .45s carried by some of the older Lost Soldiers—shake.

Chalmers nodded. It was the healer. The one who'd treated both Kenla and the hetman. She coughed, blood touching her lips, a knife gleaming wetly in her left fist.

Jackson fell to his knees, then across the woman's legs.

"What the hell?" Chalmers grunted.

* * *

## AUKSKANIS MOUNTAINS: MISSION DAY 051

Chalmers grunted and slowed the buggy to a crawl as sentries waved to him from a guard post located just below the crest of the pass. They'd been under observation for at least the last ten kilometers, from well-concealed watch posts they only knew of because of the images the SpinDogs had given Murphy and by roving patrols they had caught glimpses of once or twice in the hours it had taken them to come this far.

A large man, with dreadlocks, a broad, scarred face, and wearing the loose, flowing tunic and pants that seemed something of a uniform for the indigs, came out of a rampart-like arrangement of felled timber, earth, and stone. He barked something that Chalmers lost the meaning of somewhere between the thick accent and missing teeth.

Chalmers put the buggy in neutral and braked to a stop but kept the motor running.

Jackson smiled and called back in the same language, "We're here to see the chief."

The man smiled, showing dark spaces where his front teeth should be. "The Kedlakis-Ur waits for you with son and daughter at tent *something* the *something*."

"Can get this in?" Jackson asked, gesturing at the buggy.

The guard nodded and said, "I send warrior with you to make sure you not *something* on *something*."

"Understood," Jackson said. Chalmers really didn't want to think how hard his life would be without a good partner. Jackson truly had the gift of tongues.

"Mayal, you go with *something*. Guide past the *something*."

A skinny warrior—Chalmers did a quick double-take as he made out the fine features and beardless chin—woman came out of the defenses and eyed the buggy suspiciously.

Jackson smiled and waved the woman to the back seat, which she promptly climbed into. Chalmers eyed her in the rear-view. The woman named Mayal held herself tightly and didn't strap in until Jackson leaned back and showed her how to work the three-point restraint. She seemed a lot younger perched nervously in the unfamiliar seat, one of the long-barreled single-shot rifles favored by better-equipped nomads held muzzle-down between her knees. She smelled of nomad, too. A not entirely unpleasant tickling of the nose that fell somewhere between sweat and sage.

Once she was situated, Chalmers put the buggy into gear and eased past the guard post. About a hundred yards on, the saddle at the top of the pass narrowed to the width of a football field.

Mayal tapped his right shoulder and pointed to the right.

Chalmers obeyed, and, after they covered about twenty yards on the new heading, she tapped his other shoulder, pointing to the left. He changed direction, but she tapped him again, directing a harder left.

"Shit!" Jackson said, looking down.

"What?" Chalmers asked, taking his foot off the gas.

"Didn't you listen to the guard boss?" Jackson spat.

"I fucking listened, man," Chalmers answered, mildly angry at lying. "I just couldn't understand him past the lisp."

"Right," Jackson said, shaking his head and gesturing at the ground to the right, "Pits, man. Covered pits. Big enough to swallow a rider...or us."

"Jesus." Chalmers made sure to drive slowly for the next ten minutes as Mayal guided them through another series of changes of direction. When she relaxed in her seat, he relaxed. By then, though, they'd climbed to the top of the pass and turned up a defile that was only a few feet wider than the buggy.

They drove out of the shadow of the defile into a larger box canyon, a narrow, side-hugging shelf that descended to the canyon floor, which held the tents of the encampment.

Chalmers nervously kept the driver's side wheel next to the wall of the canyon. The last thing he wanted was to go over the edge and down the two hundred yards or so to the floor. He whistled after a moment. What he'd first taken for a scattering of only twenty-odd tents resolved, after a more careful study, into nearly a hundred.

"This is a freaking town, not a camp," Jackson said, his eyes on a forge being worked under an awning of one of the larger pavilions, located hard by the spring that had presumably helped carve the network of draws and canyons that made up the territory Chalmers and Jackson had just come through.

Their engine noise attracted the interest of a great number of the locals, who paused to watch them as Chalmers navigated the narrow track. Some started moving onto the trail head.

"Major Murphy did say something about the tribal leadership summoning the clans after the beating Moorefield gave the J'Stull."

Jackson nodded, but the sergeant didn't otherwise answer. Chalmers could see the sergeant's fingers twitching as he kept counting tents.

"Figure a family a tent, a hundred tents…" Chalmers mused. "What do you figure, one or two military age males per family?"

"Stop throwing numbers at me. I'm trying to count."

Chalmers shut up.

"Jesus," Jackson said after another minute. "There's ninety-six tents in view. Call it at least two hundred, two hundred and fifty, military age *people*," Jackson said, hiking a thumb at the woman in the back seat.

"I wonder how things ended up that way," Chalmers said. "No religion's saying it's a no-no, maybe?"

"Gotta think it's more than that," Jackson said, sounding thoughtful. "They inherited their way of living from the Ktor. And I think the decline in tech was faster and mentally easier to accept than the disintegration of social norms."

Chalmers chuckled.

Jackson shot him a look. "What?"

"You talk a good game, but I think you had more schooling than you let on," Chalmers said, navigating the last turn of the trail before reaching the bottom of the canyon.

"I had occasion to read a lot," Jackson said, looking sidelong at his partner, "and a library card is free, yo!"

Chalmers was prevented from talking shit when Mayal pointed at a nearby tent and said, "There."

A large number of indigs were already gathered around their destination, with more arriving every moment. The crush of bodies forced Chalmers to slow to a crawl. All ages were represented, though the people were generally thinner and just a little shorter than most 20th Century Americans. Everyone was armed in one way or another, the richest having some form of rifle and smoothbore muskets for the slightly less affluent.

"Lots of bandoliers filled with shells, almost enough to equip the extras on *Blazing Saddles*," Chalmers said nervously. The crowd was parting for them, but slowly, and everyone was eyeballing them like they wanted to cut a flank steak from their bodies.

"Not that many bandoliers in that flick. You're thinking *Three Amigos*, man," Jackson said, nerves making his voice high.

"That the one with Chevy Chase?"

"Yup."

"Dammit," Chalmers said, shaking his head. "I always get them mixed up."

"Good way to keep 'em separate is to count n-bombs. Not an n-bomb in *Three Amigos,* while *Blazing Saddles* has them all over the place. Then again, that's 'cause there's not a single black person in *Three Amigos*, and Mel's always interested in punching people in the face with their own racism and bigotry. Love that old bastard."

"Probably dead, now, though," Chalmers said as he parked in front of their destination.

"Why you gotta be a dick, Chalmers?" Jackson shook his head. "Mel will live forever, man! *The 2000 Year Old Man* is immortal!"

"Sorry, Jacks. Guess I'm just not that nice a guy." He shut the motor down.

"At least you own it," Jackson said as a tall woman stepped from the tent. The crowd quieted. Not that they'd been that loud to begin with. The newcomer looked about forty, which meant she was likely in her mid- to early thirties. A nomad's life wasn't easy, not even for the wealthy, not unless they were filthy rich, by which point they'd carefully *chosen* to remain nomads.

"Who is the chief, again?" Chalmers asked.

"Not sure Murphy had a name for us, but the guard said Kedlakis-Ur, right?"

"Awesome."

"Just like the regular Army," Jackson said, grinning.

Shaking his head, Chalmers concealed his own smile until Jackson wasn't looking. No use letting Jackson know in just how high a regard Chalmers held the small sergeant.

\* \* \* \* \*

# Chapter Seven –
# Cry Wolf

**CLARTHU: MISSION DAY 052**

Chalmers held the small sergeant in his arms, tears streaming down his face. All he could think was that he'd gotten his only friend in the world killed.

He was still holding the sergeant when the indigs found them a few minutes after Jackson had shot their healer.

Their response to the situation was strange: they did not seem angry. Not in the least. They picked up their healer, causing her to cough up a great gout of blood. He thought sure it was her death rattle, but she was mumbling as they carried her from the storehouse. They left him almost alone and feeling entirely desolate. Almost alone because one of the villagers stayed behind. He was a thin-faced guy with a sparse beard and pockmarked cheeks. Chalmers was pretty sure he could take this local easily, even without the Beretta they hadn't bothered to confiscate. To his surprise, the man knelt and gently disengaged Chalmers' arms from around his friend.

The villager surprised the warrant officer once again by grinning at him, eyes laughing.

"What the fuck you smiling at?" Chalmers hissed. He said it in English, forgetting his debased Ktoran in the moment but trusting that, regardless of language, his tone conveyed his meaning.

Maddeningly, the man smiled more broadly and said something Chalmers didn't understand.

"Fuck you!" Chalmers snarled.

The bastard snorted and, lifting Jackson's arm at the elbow, slapped Chalmers in the face with one limp, warm hand.

Chalmers surged to his knees, spilling his friend to the ground. "You mother—"

Which is when it dawned on him that Jackson's limp hand was warm, not cold. And not cooling, either.

"He's alive?" Chalmers asked, in English.

The man grinned wider still and mimed wiping away tears, then laughed at Chalmers.

"Get your shit together, Warrant," Chalmers told himself, pressing a shaking hand to the sergeant's neck. Sure enough, a slow, steady pulse was there.

"What happened?" Chalmers asked.

"She gave him the slap of sleep. Like Kedlak," the other man said, once he'd stopped laughing. The bastard was wiping actual tears away. When Chalmers clearly had no idea what he was talking about, the man pointed a red-ochre stain on the other side of Jackson's neck from where he'd taken the pulse.

"Why did Ked have a-a head—bad"—he struggled to find the right word—"a head-*hurt* then?" Chalmers asked, glad he hadn't touched the stuff, and angry the man had given no warning.

A careless shrug. "Hit head when he fell."

Chalmers wanted to choke the smirk off the man's face, not least because he'd been such an unsympathetic witness to his moment—okay, moments—of weakness.

"When will he wake?"

Another shrug. "Morning."

"Can we wake him up before?"

"Safer not to. You want help carrying to tent?"

"Yes, please."

They gathered Jackson up. Chalmers stared at Ked as they carried Jackson past, confirming he was still snoring.

"You put in good word with his sister?" asked the helpful villager.

"What?"

"I like her like you like him," the man said, nodding at the unconscious Jackson slung between them.

"What?" Chalmers, addled by his evening, simply could not comprehend what he was being told.

"Man like you," the man waggled one scarred brow, and said very slowly, "with begroag *something* juices marking his leg, has hard time looking for love, no? That's why you let begroag *something* your leg, to show you are ready for love."

Unsure what the man was talking about, Chalmers looked at his pant leg, noting for the first time the oily, glittery sheen on the fabric from just below the knee to the top of his booted foot. In short, it looked like a glittered-up and oily stripper had humped his lower leg and the top of his foot for an hour.

"What the?" Chalmers cried, dropping Jackson's arms. The unconscious man's head thumped hard on the packed earth floor, but Chalmers was too busy trying to figure out how to get the stuff off his leg without touching it to give his friend's comfort much thought.

"The scales of begroag are pretty when still moist, no?" The man was laughing again.

Furious, fed up, and just a little frightened by how little he knew of this place, these people, and these times, Chalmers stomped around swearing at the top of his lungs for the next little while. The tirade included choice words from four different languages and a couple he made up on the spot to better describe his disgust in the best possible fashion. It didn't achieve anything other than making him feel better, but that was enough. Eventually he ran out of words, if not steam, and stomped back to the still-unconscious Jackson and the indig.

"All right, Laughing Boy, get his legs."

"Laughing Boy?" The man asked, all trace of humor gone from his face. "I am a man. Full warrior of the clan. You, who are not a full warrior, do not call me boy."

Chalmers stared at him, grinding his teeth. Eventually, he threw his hands in the air and said, an edge of hysterical laughter he hated in his voice, "If you would tell me your name, I would not have to give you insult!"

The man cocked his head, considering whether or not to continue taking umbrage. Chalmers let his hand settle on the holstered pistol at his belt, fully ready to shoot anyone who gave him the least bit more shit.

But the man's good humor returned as he smiled and said, "Artzhimaklid is my name, War Technician."

"All right, Archie, get his damn legs. Don't want another begroag to come along and decide to ride him like a pony."

"Pony? What is pony?"

"Small riding beast."

Archie chuckled at that. "Watch his head."

Navigating the narrow passage, the pair carried the unconscious man into the hetman's home and placed him on the bedding Jackson and Chalmers had set up there before the stakeout. Kenla and the hetman were still asleep. Something about her victory over the man had made them all a guest of his for however long her wounds required to heal.

*Speaking of which*…Chalmers checked and saw that Kenla had not stirred from the makeshift bed in which the healer had treated her. Wishing there was someone he could talk to other than Archie, Chalmers led the way back outside and returned to the storehouse.

It wasn't until they had Ked laid out in his own bedroll that Chalmers realized just how weird the whole situation was. Within barely twelve hours, Clarthu's four visitors had killed the hetman's son, stabbed the hetman near to death, and shot their healer. Oh, and said healer was clearly reporting their movements to the enemy while the son of the hetman had either sold something or, more alarmingly, been bought to the tune of an anti-armor weapon and ammunition.

Something was wrong. No, so many things were wrong that Chalmers couldn't sort out just what he should focus on.

* * *

### AUKSKANIS MOUNTAIN CAMP: MISSION DAY 051

"Focus on the mission," Chalmers told himself as the indigs of Kedlakis continued to gather. He tried not to shove too hard at the onlookers as he came around the buggy to stand next to the passenger side.

Being surrounded by so many armed strangers would make anyone nervous, and Chalmers already had a suspicious nature. Even if they'd had an extraction team and pair of Blackhawks ready to rain death on anyone who stepped out of line, he'd have been anxious. As it was, Captain Mara Lee—call sign "Bruce"—was supposed to be paralleling them in the next valley over, ready to come in hot should they call for her, but that was cold comfort. Chalmers respected the pilot, but even if she could get to them in two minutes, anything more than a minute was an eternity in close quarters battle. Things were so tight with the indigs that if anything popped off, they were done for.

"Is that Kedlakis-Ur?" Jackson asked Mayal, nodding in the newly-appeared woman's direction.

The young warrior nodded but quietly added, "*The* Kedlakis-Ur, yes."

Jackson glanced at Chalmers, who gave a slight nod and started pushing against the crowd to make room for his companion. The sergeant climbed out of the buggy and stood in the space provided as the Kedlakis-Ur approached. By the time he was standing next to Chalmers, the Kedlakis-Ur was before them, the crowd had parted for her without a command.

She was thick-wristed and sleekly muscled. Tall and powerfully built in the way of ranchers back home, her long, dark hair was bound in what looked like a complicated network of braids that were allowed to fall down her back after passing through a yellow stone ring. A real man-eater.

Chalmers liked the type.

"Greetings, Kedlakis-Ur," Jackson said. "I am Sergeant Jackson, and this is Warrant Officer Chalmers. We were told you are expecting us. We bring the promised gifts."

The woman studied them both for a long moment. Chalmers didn't usually feel uncomfortable when women looked at him, but there was something about this woman's regard that left him with the sense he'd been weighed and found wanting.

"I am the Kedlakis-Ur. Welcome to the camp of the Kedlak. You have my protection and welcome." The woman's voice was gravel on rose petals. The kind you wanted to hear raised in song.

Chalmers and Jackson waited for more, but the woman stood silently regarding them.

"We...ahh, have the promised gifts," Chalmers said, after the silence had stretched too long for comfort.

The woman nodded, and Chalmers gestured.

Jackson climbed into the back seat and grunted as he pulled the bag of SpinDog-approved goodies from the foot well. Never ones to trust REMFs—especially someone else's REMFs—to provide every-thing they might need, Chalmers and Jackson had both added a few hopefully high-value items from their personal rucks.

The Kedlakis-Ur gestured for a young man at her right to pick up the pack when Jackson dropped it at her feet. The youth easily hefted the pack and slung it over his shoulder, retreating toward one of the nearby tents.

The indigs crowding the Lost Soldiers began to disperse. Their steady withdrawal made Chalmers more nervous rather than less. He wasn't sure if the behavior was due to the indigs observing some unknown social formality, but it seemed odd the indigs didn't hang around to see what these outsiders were offering their chief and, ultimately, them. It made him feel as if it were Jackson and Chalmers themselves the locals had come to see…like they were a low rent freakshow that hadn't lived up to the barker's claims.

Chalmers was anxious enough that when he looked back at the Kedlakis-Ur and found her staring at him, an electric jolt ran from the base of his spine to his skull. She really was quite attractive, with eyes of a deep, burnt amber that he'd never seen the likes of before. His earlier discomfort was gone, leaving a different sort of ache in its place.

"We thank you for your protection and welcome," Chalmers mumbled, hoping he didn't misspeak. "And hope you will accept the gifts offered."

"They will no doubt prove sufficient, War Technician," the Ked-lakis-Ur said, turning away. Chalmers, released from her magnetic gaze, stumbled forward after her, noting the same delicate, sage-like scent in her wake and a very feminine sway to her hips under the wide belt she wore.

She walked them toward the tent to which the younger man had taken their offering.

Jackson nudged the warrant, giving Chalmers one of his patented "what the fuck?" looks. Chalmers just shrugged and followed the woman into her large tent.

The interior was more like one of the surgeon's barracks-tents from *M.A.S.H.* than the Arab chieftain's harem tent he'd half-expected. Sure, it was decked out with all the amenities the upper class could get, but there was still something unmistakably military— and spartan—about the interior.

They were offered seats on low benches that Chalmers recalled were multi-purposed as racks for stowing tents when on the move as well as frameworks for hasty defenses that, when filled with earth, made excellent barricades. The benches bore cushions that doubled as containers when traveling, and currently stored other fabrics and filler that could be sat upon without damaging them. Indeed, from lamps to seating, everything the nomads made for themselves had multiple purposes. It said something about their mentality that Chalmers sensed must be important.

"Be welcome in my tent," the Kedlakis-Ur said, once they were seated. "Please take food and drink."

"Thank you, but we are neither thirsty nor hungry," Chalmers said, grateful he'd retained the SpinDog briefing on this, at least. They were to refuse the first offer, and second, but refusing the third offer of food and water would give grave insult.

"Please, you must be weary from your travels, we have plenty."

"We are healthy and strong, and our travels short."

"I do not doubt it, but comfort is offered, and for it to be received would be our pleasure." She clapped her hands, and the young man who had taken charge of their bag at the buggy entered with a large, shallow, and elaborately-chased silver bowl in his hands. If the fine silverware was incongruous against the bandoliers and still-slung rifle across his back, the Kedlakis-Ur gave no sign.

"We would not deny you your pleasure," Chalmers said.

He could feel Jackson relaxing at his successful completion of the ritual, and cast his own patented look the sergeant's way, the one meant to tell his partner, "See, I'm not completely clueless."

Unaware of the silent byplay, the young man came forward and offered the bowl, which was filled with alien fruits and what looked like jerky. Chalmers took a selection of both and ate enough to, he hoped, avoid rudeness, not because of any distaste for what was offered—it was quite tasty, the fruit in particular—rather, getting a case of the R'Bak Runs was high on his list of shit to avoid, if he could. The SEAL, whatshisname, had reported it as a thing, despite the conditioning medications the SpinDogs had given them. It made sense to Chalmers there'd be something about the food that was hard on Terran digestion, given that R'Bak was a lot farther from Kansas than the Mog, and acclimating to what the warlords had fed their guests there had put some folks in line for the latrine for days. Even the smallest amount of the wrong food could make a man wish he were dead.

He filed such concerns under, "the things a soldier had to do to survive," and moved on.

"Your messenger did not offer many details of what would be expected of us in the coming days," their host said, gracefully plucking what looked like a green grape the size of a tangerine from the bowl and biting into it.

Chalmers smiled and wished, not for the last time, that he knew more about this place and these people. "The mission changed not two days ago. Even we did not know what was to be done until Major Murphy told us."

"You do not answer the question I did not ask," she said, a broad smile lighting up those exceptional eyes.

Chalmers returned his own, more cautious grin. All his raging successes with women had been short term. Once they got to know what he was really like, they always grew to hate him. It was one of the things about this second life he hoped to change. "To be honest, we need guides who can—" he paused to be certain of the word: verb tenses were such a bitch, "—introduce us to the people of Clarthu."

"And then?" she asked, taking another bite of the fruit. The juices made her lips glisten. They were nice lips.

"Then we will find the one who reports our movements to our common enemy."

"'*We* will find?'" the Kedlakis-Ur asked, arching an eyebrow that had a thin scar running its length.

"It is hoped your guides will help us track down the spy, yes." Chalmers finished less confidently than he'd hoped, unable to gauge just what this woman wanted from him.

"The people of Clarthu will not look kindly on us *something* in their *something*," she said, too quickly for him to understand.

Chalmers glanced in puzzlement at Jackson, who said, "Can you clarify, Kedlakis-Ur? Do you mean they will not like us, collectively, interfering, or that they will not like *your* people interfering?"

The Kedlakis-Ur finished her fruit and licked the last of the juices from her fingers before responding. "Both. But they will not want interference from my people. We are seen as *something* to them." When she saw that Chalmers had lost her meaning, she explained the term, "A thing or person that is needed, but not wanted."

"I see," Chalmers said.

"I will give you the help you ask for. The guides will be told to try and avoid *something* the villagers," Chalmers figured out the word he'd missed as "antagonize" a beat or two after she said it.

"Our thanks, Kedlakis-Ur."

"For now, take your ease. You will sleep here."

"Do you not want to see our gifts?"

She waved dismissively. "It can wait until after you've rested. I will select your guides while you rest." She stood with the same fluid grace she'd exhibited from the first.

Chalmers got an elbow in the ribs as he watched her leave.

"What?" he complained, rubbing his side and glaring at Jackson.

"Please don't let a need to dip your wick get us in trouble, man."

"I won't," Chalmers said, swallowing against a suddenly-dry throat. "She's something, though."

"No doubt." Jackson's smile cracked his concerned expression. "No doubt. Still, we need to watch our shit. These waters are deeper than Lake Michigan, and we don't know half what we should."

Chalmers nodded and cocked his head. "Speaking of which, you notice she didn't seem too concerned with the bribe we offered?"

"Nope. Definitely has her own reasons for helping us."

"We should report in; let Murphy know we've made contact, and that she's agreed to assist us."

"Copy that. You want to, or should I?"

"Go ahead," Chalmers said, looking out the tent flap in hopes of catching another glimpse of the Kedlakis-Ur.

"Quit thinking with that dipshit between your legs, Chalmers. You'll get us both killed."

"I won't jeopardize the mission, man," Chalmers said, earnestly.

Jackson looked askance at him.

"What?"

"Man, what the fuck is up with you?"

"What?" Chalmers said, more defensively than he meant to. The genuine concern in Jackson's voice made the man's question a real one, not a jab of their usual banter, to be deflected and laughed off.

"Time was you'd have told me to go fuck myself and gone on to get us in a world of shit. It was how you rolled."

"Well," Chalmers said uncomfortably, "I'm trying to change."

The reply silenced Jackson, but only for a moment. He muttered something Chalmers couldn't quite make out.

Chalmers thought about letting it ride but remembered the promise he'd made to himself. "What was that?"

Jackson's expression was a cracked mask of barely-suppressed emotion. He did an even worse job of controlling his voice, which throbbed with rage. "Now, Chalmers? *Now?* You choose now to change? I'd have thought you might have made better choices before. Before we were in this—this…situation. You see, Chalmers, I know. I fucking *know.*"

Chalmers couldn't answer, knowing his partner's anger was fully justified, that he—the man he'd been before—fully deserved it, and he could only begin to pay the bill his old ways had run up among his friends, family, and colleagues. He sat silent, hoping Jackson would unload, yet desperate his partner would not explode.

"I *know,* Chalmers," Jackson repeated, jabbing a finger hard into Chalmers' chest. "Murphy told me when I woke up. I *know* I wouldn't have even been on that God-forsaken helo if it weren't for your shitty play with that warlord. I *know* you fucked me. The only thing that stopped me from putting a bullet in your head when we woke up was the fact you were in it with me, and I kinda hoped you might catch a bullet meant for me. More than that, though, I wanted the option of fucking ending you myself if you fucked up again. That, and my momma taught me it's always better the devil you know than the devil you don't." Jackson's tirade was getting loud, but Chalmers dared not tell the sergeant to lower his voice.

"And!" Jackson nearly shouted the word, eyes wild. "And if there was ever half a chance of surviving this fucked up situation it would be helped by knowing the man beside me, even a shithead like you. And even knowing just *how* his shit floats, you asshole!"

Scarred hands drew into tight, angry fists as Jackson lowered his voice and rasped on, "But, God help me...but I've also come to realize you know how to paddle up Shit's Creek like no one else. And...and..." The sergeant heaved in a great, shaking breath before releasing it more slowly and continuing, "And...the way I see things, that's what we need to survive right now: someone who knows how to paddle."

Chalmers, overwhelmed with an unfamiliar emotion he eventually identified as gratitude, nodded and looked away from his partner's still-smoldering gaze.

"Dick," Jackson said.

Chalmers nodded, meeting his partner's gaze again. "Trying to be better, man."

"Whatever, man, just make sure you don't fucking forget to paddle while you're trying. Paddling against the shit is the one thing that's kept you alive so far," Jackson grunted roughly.

\* \* \*

## CLARTHU: MISSION DAY 053

Jackson grunted roughly as he sat bolt upright, then shouted, "Whotoleyoutoputhathere!"

Chalmers snorted. "You having crazy butt sex in your sleep again, Jackson?"

"Only with yo momma," Jackson muttered, scrubbing his face with his hands. "Wait, what the hell? Did I kill someone last night?"

"No, Kemosabe, you did not. Not for lack of trying, though."

"I missed? He was so close."

Despite the absence of the young man who knew the full story, Chalmers decided not to lie and instead took the high road and said, "Nope. You tagged them. Right in the chest."

Just because Chalmers wasn't lying didn't mean he had to admit to Jackson that he had missed so badly as to endanger them both with the ricochet, or that he didn't want to distract him from the impact of shooting someone, something Jackson had only had to do once before, if Chalmers recalled correctly. And that hadn't been a woman. Not that it should matter when you are threatened with deadly force, but some folks needed reassurance they wore the white hats, even when they were entirely within their rights to defend themselves. And some guys, Chalmers included, had a hard time reconciling harming a woman with being the good guy.

"In the chest? And he ain't dead?"

"Not yet," Chalmers said with a shrug. "And if the way these freakish villagers are acting is any indication, she's likely to live."

"No shit?"

"No shit," Chalmers answered, glad Jackson had missed his gender slip.

"How?"

"A couple of followers—I think they're apprentices or something—took charge and have been working on her ever since."

"Surgery?"

Chalmers shrugged. "I guess. I had to drag you in here while you were sleeping on the job."

"Wait...*her*? I shot some chick?"

Cursing inwardly, Chalmers qualified his partner's statement. "No, you shot an *attacker*, thinking they were about to kill you."

"The healer?"

"The healer," Chalmers confirmed.

Jackson shook his head in confusion. "So, the villagers weren't pissed?"

"I know, right?" Chalmers said it with feeling. He'd sat up all night spinning his wheels between concern for Jackson and wondering when someone would come to kill them both.

"But one of our party offs the hetman's kid and then I shoot their healer?"

"Yeah, it's starting to make me think there is something seriously wrong with these people."

"Starting?"

"Jacks, I am freaked out. Haven't slept all night."

"Wait...what did she knock me out with? I don't feel like I was cracked in the head," Jackson said, hands investigating his shaved skull.

"She used some kind of drug on you."

Jackson looked more confused, not less. "Bullshit. That kinda shit only happens in movies."

"What's that, you getting knocked out by a woman? 'Cause I'm pretty sure there was tha—"

Jackson interrupted him. "Naw, man, a drug knocking someone out that quick." The smaller man stood up and cracked his neck by the simple expedient of grabbing his head in both hands and twisting one way and then the other.

"I don't know; doesn't chloroform work that way?"

"Sure, but it's risky as hell. Killed a lot of people even when used by doctors." Jackson pulled his pistol, press-checked it, and popped the magazine. "I don't feel any the worse for wear."

"No shit?" Chalmers asked.

"No shit." He looked a question at Chalmers, who gestured at the pack behind the bedroll Jackson had been lying on.

"Okay, but why is it important?"

Jackson shrugged as he rummaged in the pack for the box of ammunition. He palmed a cartridge and closed his pack up. "Aside from my mouth tasting a bit of ass, I don't feel any real side effects, and any medic who can do that for our wounded would be worth their weight in gold."

Chalmers nodded. "I see. Well, guess we oughta hope you didn't kill her then?"

The question elicited another shrug from Jackson as he slid the fat .45 cartridge into the magazine. "Street rules: come at me, I go at you. Happened before, will happen again. Street rules." He slid the magazine into the well and tapped it with the heel of his left hand to make sure it was properly seated, then holstered up.

"Copy that," Chalmers said, wondering again what kind of life Jackson had come to the Army from.

Jackson crossed his arms over his chest then said, "Besides, her doctor's bag probably has enough of whatever she used on me and maybe even more useful stuff. We can take samples back to the major."

"And then what?" Chalmers asked. "The SpinDogs aren't as advanced as the freakshows that brought us here, and I didn't see anything that would let us synthesize tea like on the *Enterprise*."

Jackson shook his head. "Your momma never accused you a thinkin' too far ahead, did she? I want to make it past this shit-show and somehow make a life. To do that, I think we gonna need everything we can get: ideas, dope, weapons, allies, whatever. Every damn thing we can get. When you up against it, street rules apply."

"Makes sense," Chalmers said, unsure he still wanted to know what Jackson's childhood had been like. He'd always known the sergeant was smarter, a little more ruthless, a better planner, and simply a better man than he himself was, but the hard edge to Jackson's voice made Chalmers shiver. And neither the tone nor content of

Jackson's statement had been directed at him, but rather at an uncaring universe. It seemed to Chalmers at that moment that it was just possible Jackson could bend that universe to his will.

Maybe.

\* \* \* \* \*

# Chapter Eight – Mileage May Vary

### AUKSKANIS MOUNTAIN CAMP: MISSION DAY 052

**M**aybe it was the way Jackson had cleared the air, but Chalmers woke feeling pretty damn good about things. Could have been that, could also have been that he'd only had to hit the latrine once during the night, and there'd been no discernible difference in that visit to the usual, despite over-indulging in some of the local fare before bed. It was good. Halfway between Tex-Mex and some of the Palestinian food his neighbor used to make.

The stuff he'd been helpless to resist had looked like a whitish celery stalk, tasted like honeyed lemons, and smelled like really good chocolate. He'd mentioned the stuff was the perfect Valentine's Day gift, but Jackson's dark stare had forced him to put away any thoughts of trying his theory out on the Kedlakis-Ur. Their host had been generous with her time and company, and Chalmers woke to the very real desire to spend more time in the camp, if only to discover whether the Kedlakis-Ur was truly a man-eater or just looked like one.

Seeking diversion from the nascent erection brought on by thoughts of the tribal leader, Chalmers sat up and looked around.

Jackson was standing just outside the tent, drinking something hot from an earthen mug.

Chalmers rubbed the sleep from his eyes and joined the shorter man under the awning.

"Morning," Jackson said.

"Morning," Chalmers returned, yawning. The nights were short, but blessedly cool, especially in the highlands, and the lingering cold did as much to wake Chalmers as the mug of hot liquid Jackson handed him.

"Any new instructions from command?" Chalmers asked. He sniffed, glad the fragrant tea covered the scent of stale sweat and dust that had permeated his clothes.

"Only to repeat that the timetable is tight, and we will need to move fast once in Clarthu. The unit left Camp Stark yesterday at 0500 and is on schedule."

Chalmers nodded. "We really don't know enough about the villagers to guarantee even a qualified success, do we?"

"Not yet, no. I plan on picking the guide's brain while we drive."

"Speaking of which, any idea who the Kedlakis-Ur is sending with us?"

"I think we're about to find out," Jackson answered, nodding toward the three figures just emerging from the chief's tent. The Lost Soldiers had been hosted there for another, later meal after their initial interview, and then treated to entertainment from a pair of young singers accompanied by the Kedlakis-Ur on a stringed instrument that looked positively medieval. Jackson and Chalmers had nodded along like two Catholics at a Baptist church on Sunday, unfamiliar with the words, but grooving to the music and feeling the sentiment. When the party had ended, the pair of them had been escorted here, to what they presumed was a guest tent of sorts, as it had none of the embroidery and decoration the Kedlakis-Ur's had, but was comfortable enough.

One of the figures accompanying the Kedlakis-Ur was the young man who had served them the night before, the other was a woman about the same age as the man. Both were armed with breech-loading rifles and wore matching expressions of, if not anger, then intensity. As they drew closer Chalmers realized the pair looked a lot alike, though they could just have a strong clan resemblance rather than be siblings. Their erect carriage and self-assurance gave the impression of competence.

Then again, Chalmers had always made a point of *looking* competent, too. Especially when fucking around.

He supposed that in this case, though, appearances would not be deceiving. Those that had to hunt, gather, and fight to survive were less likely to successfully hide any failings. He dimly recalled some nomad group on Earth leaving those too old or infirm to make river crossings and such-like behind to die.

"Your guides," the Kedlakis-Ur said, drawing him from his observations.

Chalmers put his tea down and smiled at her. "I thank the tribe, you, and our guides for the gifts of your aid."

She cocked her head, lovely eyes narrowed on him. "The tribe is not involved. Solely the Kedlak."

"I beg pardon. I misspoke." Chalmers said the words without knowing what, exactly, he'd said that was incorrect. He'd thought the Kedlak were the tribe. He suppressed the urge to glance at Jackson and decided to shut the hell up. Clan politics, he decided.

The Kedlakis-Ur waved a hand. "There is nothing to pardon. My *something* will see you to Clarthu and help you uncover the traitor."

"Thank you," he said, restraining the urge to hit on her. Much as he wanted to chat her up, now was not the time. Not for the new, better Chalmers, anyway. Old Chalmers would have followed where this attraction led at the expense of just about anything.

"Travel easily and lightly," she said. The Kedlakis-Ur then turned to the guides and nodded once to each, repeating the benediction. The bows they gave her were the most formal thing Chalmers had seen from an indig thus far.

The Kedlakis-Ur walked away, Chalmers trying not to stare after her in case it offended the young pair.

"Head's up," Jackson said, shoving Chalmers' bag into the warrant's hands with a quelling look that made the older man wonder what he'd done now.

He loaded the buggy while Jackson topped off the tanks from the jerry cans. Their guides looked on, impassive, as the partners prepared for travel. The rest of the camp paid them no more attention than they had the night before.

"A little less than one and a half cans left, Chalmers," Jackson said, the impact of one knuckle drawing a muted bong from the partially-empty jerry can.

"Copy that. Should be plenty, so long as we don't have to fight sand or something." He looked a question at the guide.

"No sand," the guide said, shaking his head. "No big rocks. Some small gravels when we get down the *something,* and then green lands to Clarthu."

"Green lands, eh? Sounds nice," Jackson said, looking at the sere beiges, browns, and grays of the mountains surrounding the camp. "Though I suppose, growing up here, anything would look green."

Chalmers checked the tautness of the tie-downs keeping their packs in place, slung his M-14, and hustled to claim the driver's seat. He really enjoyed driving the buggy. Driving it made him feel both useful and in active command of his own destiny. In control of something that was, in fact, hard to manage. Like exerting control over his lifelong inclination to lie and fuck things up, only safer.

His rush caused the slung M-14 to bang into the steering wheel and shoved him off balance.

Or maybe *not* so much safer, after all. Murphy's Law always found a way of levelling those who started thinking too highly of themselves or their skills. Flushing, Chalmers removed the weapon, carefully slipped it into the rifle scabbard between the seats, and secured it.

"What?" asked Jackson with a grin. "I thought you were getting ready to lay on some dumbass redneck shit, driving with a gun in one hand like a wild man."

\* \* \*

### CLARTHU: MISSION DAY 053

Grinning like a wild man, a villager trotted toward the partners, a bottle in one hand.

The partners had walked the village from one end to the other. Ostensibly searching for Ked—who they'd left near Clarthu's main gate—but they were both hoping for some clue to leap up and tell them just what the hell was going on.

As the running local approached, Chalmers smiled, asked "For us?" and reached toward the bottle.

The villager swerved to avoid the warrant officer, shooting him a dirty look as he trotted the rest of the way to the gate, where he immediately handed the flask to Ked. Their guide had a leather strap holding a bandage to the wound on his head from the previous night's misadventures.

"Was that the good stuff?" Chalmers asked absently, watching their guide talk easily, casually to the newcomer and a couple of the villagers guarding the main drag into town. The young nomad took a deep swig from the bottle.

"Is it the 'good stuff'? Good stuff?" Jackson's laugh was a derisive bark. "There's no good stuff. Not here."

"You know what I mean," Chalmers said. He gestured at Ked. "What the hell is going on here, you think?"

Jackson shook his head. "I ain't sure. Something stinks, though."

Ked's smiling face was suddenly painted a bright, wet red.

"Holy—" Chalmers shouted, gaping at the man that had been standing next to Ked. A good part of the man's face was gone, or at least mangled beyond all recognition.

Chalmers blinked, his brain catching up even as the sound of the shot reached his ears: a large caliber bullet had entered the back of the man's head blasting out a spray of skull, teeth, and skin. It was his blood, not paint, that had splashed all over Ked.

"Down!" Jackson bellowed, already yanking Chalmers into a crouch beside him.

That part of his brain not reeling from the sudden violence and death in front of them was amazed at how fast Jackson's reflexes were. His partner was already kneeling beside the front wall of the hetman's place, scanning for the shooter.

Ked was also in a crouch and moving to cover even as something raised a puff of brick dust against the wall beside him.

This time the sound of the sniper's shot was drowned out as Jackson opened up right next to him. The four fast rounds from his M-14 made Chalmers jump. The warrant officer knew his hearing wouldn't be the same after a few more close shots, but couldn't care less, so long as Jackson kept the sniper from shooting again.

Chalmers risked a quick look over the wall at the area Jackson was firing upon. A largish stand of the tree-like grasses he'd almost hit on the way in lined a juncture of two of the irrigation canals about a hundred and fifty yards from the village. It wasn't much as cover, but it had obviously provided great concealment up until the moment the sniper had fired. Now, though, a thin, whitish cloud of smoke marked the sniper's hide.

Another puff of smoke. Chalmers ducked. Someone yelped off to the left and the sound of the gunshot rolled in a heartbeat later.

Chalmers risked another look as Jackson returned fire again. A sapling-sized blade of the tree-grass fell a yard or so above the smoke. Jackson was shooting straight.

He ducked back down as another puff of smoke erupted, this one from a few yards to the right of the earlier, slowly-dissipating ones. Either there were multiple shooters, or the sniper had displaced a few yards.

Chalmers had no idea where the round went because he was busy flogging his brain for an approach to the stand that wouldn't get him shot. One of the canals ran parallel to the low stone wall surrounding the village, flowing from the millrace that powered the village's mill.

Ked and a couple of the villagers with him thumped backs-first into the wall to the left of the partners. One raised his rifle—no, musket—and fired. A flash in the pan, then nothing. The man cursed and lowered his weapon, which decided to discharge at that very moment. Thankfully the round didn't hit anyone, just buried itself in the mud brick in front of him, but the misfire did throw the gun out of the frightened villager's grip.

"Jesus," Chalmers grunted.

Ked's breechloader proved more reliable as the grinning nomad *banged* a round downrange at the enemy and dropped back to reload.

"Who's shooting at us?" Chalmers shouted.

"Enemy," Ked shouted back.

*Rather unhelpful,* Chalmers thought. "Try and leapfrog up to them?" Chalmers asked Jackson, hoping the answer wasn't yes.

"Don't like the odds without a better base of fire and some grenades," Jackson said, far more calmly than Chalmers felt. The sergeant displaced a couple yards along the wall, popped up, and fired another fast semi-auto flurry before ducking back behind cover.

"What you want me to do?"

"Fuck if I—" A ragged clatter of gunfire from the far end of the village cut him off.

"What the hell!" Chalmers blurted, swinging his head that way.

A flat *CRUMP* came next, scaring the shit out of him.

"Mortar!" he shouted, unnecessarily.

"Get the buggy under cover!" Jacks shouted, his cheek still along the receiver of the M-14 as he laid down fire.

"*Cover? Cover?* There is no fucking cover!" Chalmers screamed even as he started toward the vehicle. It seemed to require far too much time in the open to cover the ground between buggy and wall, though that was probably because of the insufficient air wheezing through his fear-constricted windpipe and the fact that he couldn't seem to stand up straight.

*CRUMP!* Another explosion threatened to deafen him. Dust and smoke. Still on the far side of the village, thankfully.

"Jesus!" Chalmers screamed, jumping the last few yards to the buggy. He dropped the key trying to get it out, get in, and get the vehicle started all in one go. He bent, retrieved the key, and jammed it in, starting the motor.

Jackson dropped into the passenger seat. "Jesus!" Chalmers screamed; the sound startled from his lips.

"Not Jesus! Just drive!" Jacks shouted.

*CRUMP!*

The engine revved high before Chalmers remembered to slam it into gear. They shuddered into motion.

An absurd feeling of relief struck Chalmers. Moving targets were harder to hit, and they could always simply get the hell out of Dodge if push came to shove.

"They must have only the one tube," Jackson shouted. "Get us out of town."

Only too happy to comply, Chalmers worked the buggy into second gear as they blew past the last building of the village proper and out onto the beaten earth path that led toward the closest satrap city.

"The shooter!" Jackson's shout was nearly lost in the *CRUMP!* of another shell exploding, but his pointing arm was clear enough.

The track they were on curved away from the enemy positions. Chalmers hadn't driven this way and wasn't sure how to get across the—he counted quickly—two canals to the stand of giant grasses Jackson was pointing at. Then he saw there was another canal that connected the two, like the cross of a giant H. The near juncture of the H was close, maybe two hundred yards. Conscious of the adrenaline pushing him to go faster, Chalmers tried to keep the buggy at a safe speed, but the noise of repeated gunshots and explosions made him want to crush the accelerator with the heaviest lead foot across seven star systems.

It looked like the far end of the village was the focus of the assault while this end was pinned down by a squad or war party or whatever.

"Where the hell you going, Chalmers?"

*CRUMP!*

"Gonna go out and around, come back at them from behind," Chalmers shouted, the words carrying them almost to the place where the connecting canal ran under a wooden bridge. He went off road for a better look at the canal.

"Can we use it?" Chalmers shouted at Jackson.

"Shallow enough," Jacks shouted back.

"The slope?" Chalmers asked, figuring Jackson was answering how deep the water was, not the slope.

"Oh. Steep, but where the wall meets the bottom looks gentle." He cupped a hand to show Chalmers.

"Fuck it," Chalmers said. Not wanting to roll the buggy, he slowed and angled the vehicle so as to drop into the canal as smoothly as possible. Even with his careful approach, the buggy nearly tipped. The violent change of direction made their shoulders slam together, the impact nearly launching the lighter Jackson out of his seat. Chalmers grabbed him one-handed by the web harness and yanked him back to safety.

The buggy chugged, nearly stalling as his foot came off the accelerator with no downshift. By some miracle he managed a gear change before they hit the sluggish flow at the bottom of the canal and watery mud rocketed up all about them. He let the water slow them to a walking pace as the buggy's fat wheels pushed matching bow waves of stinking mud before them. With any luck, the bad guys would think they wrecked. Failing that, Chalmers guessed the canal would mask their engine noise, make it harder to tell where they were in relation to the attackers. Unless there was someone in the canal with them.

A wide-eyed and cursing Jackson rested his M-14 muzzle in the foot well and started putting the four-point restraint on. Steering with his knees. Chalmers followed suit, or tried to.

"All right, we follow this to the junction, then turn right and we're behind the bastards," Chalmers grunted. He lifted his ass to get at one half of the buckle he'd been sitting on. "We go straight at them and we nosedive into the next canal."

Jackson nodded.

Chalmers clipped in and was suddenly breathing easier. Then the absolute absurdity of the feeling of safety he had from putting on a seatbelt on in the middle of a gunfight struck him, making him giggle madly.

Jackson spared him an old fashioned look.

"Buckle up, bitches!" a smiling Chalmers brayed, hammering the accelerator. Rooster tails of sludge shot up, behind, and all around them.

Jackson, either buying into his madness or too busy holding onto the chicken bar to say anything, just nodded. Nodded and, once the acceleration steadied, raised his M-14 to rest the forestock on the roll cage's crossbar.

*CRUMP!*

The crackle of gunfire was muted by the steep banks around them but still accompanied their progress. They soon reached the far juncture. Chalmers turned into it, decided this canal was too deep to push along the bottom, and forded it.

They'd covered maybe a hundred yards before Chalmers started looking for a way up. If his estimate was correct, they would now be about a hundred yards west of the position from where the sniper was firing on the villagers. Close enough to take the attackers under fire, but far enough to take full advantage of the M-14's greater accuracy and higher rate of fire. He really liked the idea of coming in behind the enemy's shooters.

Chalmers eyed a spot where more earth had settled into the canal, gentling the slope considerably. He needed that easy gradient because, as it was, he had to hit the gas hard to climb the sloppy surface. The engine gave a throaty grumble as he horsed the buggy up it, mud, gravel, and loose soil ricocheting from the far side of the canal in their wake.

"Fuck," Jackson said without heat, wiping the M-14's receiver clear of muck.

Unsure whether to blast out of the canal or ease his way, Chalmers dithered so long he did neither in the end. The front of the buggy dropped flat as they crested the top and bounced down onto the field, revealing three men crouched behind a tripod-looking thing Chalmers required a moment to identify.

"Mortar!" Chalmers bellowed, flooring it.

Two of the men, mouths round Os of surprise, reached for their weapons as the partners bore down on them at twenty-five and accelerating. Chalmers couldn't tell what the third guy was doing.

Jackson pointed and fired a few rounds, but only succeeded in giving his partner an earful, as far as Chalmers could tell.

Chalmers redlined it. He didn't bother to shift into second. Best not to if you were about to hit something. He tried not to think about what he was about to do.

Two of the mortar men figured it out, though, and tried to jump aside. One made it, though it didn't make any difference as the buggy crashed first into the rest of the crew, then into the mortar, which, in turn, was flung off its plate, crushing the third man's chest. He went down in a welter of blood, an oblong, finned object spinning in a lazy arc from his hands.

Chalmers slewed the buggy into a hard left, a last-ditch effort to keep himself between Jackson and the expected explosion. He was only partially successful as the dead loader's burden struck the ground and exploded with what Chalmers hoped was the final *CRUMP!* of the afternoon. Hot, hard needles traced lines along his arm, cheek, and shoulder closest to the blast, while his chest rattled with the shockwave.

The buggy, which he decided deserved a name after today's action, barely slowed. Something sounded wrong, but Chalmers couldn't be sure if it was just his abused ears shrieking their death song to his brain or actual damage to the motor. It wasn't until he tried to draw breath to laugh in relief that he realized what was making that alarming rattle: his own breathing. Well, maybe the motor was fucked up, too, but he was really having trouble getting his wind.

"Threat right!" Jackson shouted.

Chalmers turned the buggy—had to decide on a name for her, and sooner rather than later—hard in that direction. His estimate had been off: they were about four hundred yards from the mill and closer to two hundred from the tree-grass stand from which the attackers had started their ambush. Five or six warriors were still sheltered behind the rootballs of the stuff as they fired at the village, but were turning to face the growling mechanical beast that had done for their mortar team.

He watched one warrior raise his rifle and saw the puff of smoke. Chalmers supposed the shot was a miss, given the lack of a whistle, thump, or thud. Then again, his ears were truly fucked, so there was no telling.

The field was a reasonably flat couple of acres on a mild diagonal approach to the enemy position, allowing Chalmers to build some speed. He slammed the buggy—or maybe "The Beast?" Naw, sounded too masculine—into second gear, gathering speed despite the atonal complaint of steel on steel somewhere in either the gearbox or engine.

Taking advantage of the comparatively level ground, Jackson took aim as best he could and started shooting.

The guy who'd made a try for them fell. Whether shot or stumbling as he scrambled for cover, Chalmers couldn't say.

"Rumblekins," Chalmers muttered.

"What?" Jackson said, reloading with a speed and skill Chalmers knew he couldn't have matched. Hell, Jackson himself would probably be amazed at how smoothly he was able to manage the process once they got through this.

"Name—" Chalmers coughed. The pain was excruciating. He decided this coughing thing was excessive and unpleasant. He would not allow it to happen again.

"What?" Jackson asked again.

"Names for the buggy," Chalmers answered, sure his partner wasn't listening, because the sergeant was busy servicing targets again. "Beefeater," he muttered to himself past wet lips. He licked without thinking, tasting copper and salt instead of the muddy water he'd expected. "Nah," he decided, patting the wheel. "You ain't ginned up, are you, girl?"

*Oh!*

"Man-eater!" The mad cackle that followed the thought ended on a painful cough that left him slumped in the seat, wondering where the last little while had gone.

He heard Jackson shouting, but his partner wasn't in the passenger seat anymore. There was a flurry of shots from his left, not the sharp cracks of the M14's 7.62 NATO ammunition, but the more throaty booms of Jackson's .45.

Chalmers wanted to help, tried to get out, but found he couldn't. Reality kept blinking in and out, like a light switch played with by a sadistic five year old. He struggled mindlessly for far too long before realizing what the problem was. He fumbled with the buckle on the four-point restraint, his shaking fingers strangely cold.

He looked for Jackson, waiting—no, *wanting*—to hear a crack or two about how shitty his coordination was, and instead saw his death standing a few yards away. It was the warrior that had first shot at them a million years ago but less than five minutes of clock time. The raider dropped the great yawning blackness of his gun's muzzle to point at Chalmers' chest.

Reality stuttered again.

The warrant smiled redly. "Fucking shoot straight."

"Fuck you!" Jackson shrieked, leaping out from between two monstrous blades of grass. Chalmers watched, fascinated, as the pistol in his partner's hand barked and bounced, its big slide racking back and forth.

A great blossom of pain bloomed and grew to a full flower of agony rooted in the left side of Chalmers' chest. As he closed his eyes against it, he really wished his last words had been something pithy. Something worthy for his partner to remember, if not with pride, then at least with a smile. Not something that would piss the little guy off. Chalmers had done enough of that. He was trying to do better.

\* \* \*

## CAMP STARK: MISSION DAY 0??

"Do better!" Jackson's angry shout was muffled.

"I'm doing muh best, Sergeant," the man's accent was pure Missouri redneck, "But do you see an X-ray machine here? We barely know what we're dealing with when it comes to the alien fungus 'n shit. An' that shit they'uns did to close up'n his wounds don't quite track with what'n I learnt in school, unnerstan'?"

Alien fungus? A cold thrill of fear ran down Chalmers' spine. He tried to clear away whatever was covering his ears, only to discover he couldn't move his arms. He tried to speak, at least mumble, but found his mouth full of something.

"Fuck you, man," Jackson shouted. "Worst Army doctor ever!"

"Imma corpsman, not a doctor, *boy.*"

"Boy? *Boy?*" Jackson's voice went very high, very fast.

Chalmers' grin made something wet and hot trickle down the side of his head. He kept grinning anyway. From the ascending tone of Jackson's question, someone was about to get *very* messed up. Just because he was short, people tended to think they could get away with shit around Jackson. They were wrong.

He heard a clatter and a surprised yelp. Then, far more quietly: "You apologize, you cracker motherfucker or I'll break every bone in your goddamn hand."

"Look, I ain't even a doctor, just a corpsman!" the other man whined, the last parts of the sentence run together by both pain and a fervent desire to end it.

"Apologize, Cracker."

"I'msorrysosorryplease."

"Sorry, *Sergeant*."

"SosorrySergeant," the man moaned.

"That's better. See how easy that was?" A faint noise, another moan, then, "See to my partner, you cracker, or I'll see to you."

"Yes, Sergeant."

There followed a few minutes of fussing and tending from the medic, corpsman, whatever, whom Chalmers dimly remembered as some Vietnam-era redneck with a full set of tattoos and teeth that hadn't been a full set since shortly after his twelve year molars had come in. The medic or corpsman or whatever left quite quickly after that.

Chalmers tried to say something again, but not only had his mouth been stuffed, they'd wound something around his jaw. He didn't remember anything hitting him in the head enough to break any bones, but then the boxer never saw the punch that knocked him out, did he? Fear made his heart race. Was he gonna look like the Elephant Man? Uglier? He'd never considered himself model-pretty, but he'd known himself to possess a certain dark, rakish charm.

He heard what sounded like a stool being dragged over, and then Jackson's voice, clearer now that he was closer. "Hey, partner. You awake?"

Chalmers' attempt to answer came out more like a whining moan than the manly grunt he'd been trying for.

"Hey, that's good," Jackson said.

Chalmers could hear the lie in his voice.

"You lost a lot of blood, and if it weren't for another one of those Clarthu healers, we'd have lost you in those first hours. As it was, they had a hell of a time putting you back together. And now, Chalmers, there's this whole other thing…" Jackson trailed off, clearly at a loss for how to tell his partner his face was being eaten by an alien fungus.

"Hwww lnnng?"

"How long? Well, let me think. Shit, better part of two weeks, more or less? Hard to keep track."

More lost time. Chalmers thought about asking what his prognosis was, but hesitated, not really wanting to hear about how his flesh was being devoured by a mushroom.

Jackson helped distract him. "I bet you're wondering what the hell happened?"

Chalmers managed an, "Mmmmmhmmmm," that sounded a lot less emphatic than he liked. He was desperate for any kind of distraction, and his mind, never predisposed to dwell on bad news, leapt at the chance to learn what had happened in his absence.

"The hetman hadn't been paying tribute to the top dog, so the platoon-level attack we interrupted was meant to tell them who was boss."

Chalmers managed a tiny shake of his head.

"I know, right? None of the briefs said they kicked up to the satraps or their lieutenants. No, they all said Clarthu was more or less independent, that the people there could be relied on to a certain extent. And the briefs, they were correct, too—more or less—because the bosses they were supposed to be appeasing weren't

R'Baku at all, but top dogs for real. Which is to say, the SpinDogs—or rather, an isolationist faction among them."

"Ergh?" Chalmers managed, unsure whether it was painkillers, blood loss, or simply native stupidity that was preventing him understanding Jackson's explanation.

"Remember Murphy telling us there was a potential problem in that the SpinDogs were *mostly* backing us?"

"Mmmm-hmmm," Chalmers managed. His cheek was starting to itch abominably, making him bite back a sob.

"Well, it stood to reason there was another faction, one that didn't want us to interfere in their profitable and long-established dealings with the R'Baku."

"Ergh?"

"Some people can't be trusted with power," Jackson said, then swallowed loudly and let go a sigh that was tired but satisfied. "Just can't trust them at all. Want to stay there no matter what the cost is to their own organization. Apparently a group called the Hardliners are spearheading the faction that wants everything to remain status quo." He chuckled. "That means 'the same,' Chalmers."

"Fthk Uuuu," Chalmers managed.

Jackson's chuckle deepened, then became a laugh. Chalmers liked to hear it, though he didn't feel much like doing anything other than scratch away the itch that was crawling along the side of his face like shark skin rubbed the wrong way. Tears welled as Chalmers considered they might actually have to use something like sharkskin on his face to scrape the fungus out of his wounds. No more man-eaters for Chalmers. Likely no companionship ever again. Not unless he purchased it. Self-pity made silent tears flow, or try to. The bandages soaked most of them up.

Another loud swallow was followed by the sound of liquid swishing in bottle. "Damn rude of me to be drinking without you, but you can't have a drink in your condition. Something about it lowering your immune system."

Chalmers didn't even try and tell his partner to fuck off. He didn't want to aggravate the itch any further than necessary.

"Where was I?" Jackson asked after a brief wait to see if Chalmers would rise to the bait. "Oh, yeah, the Hardliners. So these fuckers realized that their source for the drugs the healers used to fix your broken ass was about to either dry up or, worse yet from their point of view, end up in the hands of the Expansionist faction: their main rivals.

"So, the Hardliners decide to make sure we failed. Spectacularly. They contacted their people on the planet—apparently they've got a network like the main SpinDog liaisons have—and activated a couple of dead drops. Murphy is pretty sure—"

"Ergk?"

"What's that? Oh, yeah, Murphy and me had a long chat after the battle and a couple of rather interesting discussions with some people here. Something went on up there, on all of the SpinDog rohabs; something heavy. Murphy was vague on specifics, but I got his drift: the shit they tried to pull here became known up there and bad blood boiled over. Anyway, the guys who attacked Clarthu may not have been following direct orders from the Hardliners—they may have had some motives of their own—but they definitely got the mortar and shells from them."

"Huuu?" Chalmers asked, the desire to know more momentarily overcoming the need to avoid more itching.

"How? Not sure of the delive—Oh, you mean how do we know?"

"Essss."

"You know how exacting their copies of our weapons are, right? That's why my .45 rattled like the ones I trained on at Basic despite the fact it was a SpinDog-made copy. Well, the mortar was straight US Army, circa Korean War, but no serial number. Not even the stamp that the SpinDogs put on their knock-offs. Meaning the Hard-liners found a way to get the plans we shared with the SpinDogs to their own fabricators—probably black-market operators among the RockHounds." Jackson shook his head. "Leastwise, that's what we think. Not a lot of real evidence left. You fucked the tube up good driving through the crew like you did."

Chalmers heard another swig and swish as Jackson drank. Silence remained in its wake; Chalmers was unable to speak and struggled to avoid recalling the feel of Man-Eater as she bucked over the bodies. He wasn't sure what Jackson was thinking, but hoped the silence was recognition of Chalmers' sacrificial act, interposing himself between Jackson and the exploding shell.

"Anyway," Jackson said after another pull on the bottle, "I think Murphy is layin' too little at the feet of the Hardliners, but he may just be taking a page from General Powell: tryin' to avoid breaking up the alliance despite the shit our allies be pulling."

"Buuuht?"

A theatrical sigh. "You talkin' too much, Chalmers. Let me get a word in edgewise, man."

"Funk uuuuu. Wheeer frm?" Chalmers managed. His bonds were loosening, which might be of concern. He probably wasn't supposed to scratch at any of his infected wounds.

"Where were the weapons from? I already tole you," Jackson was slurring a bit now, the drink obviously taking effect.

"Mnnn."

"Oh, the men were militia from the villages in the regions north of Clarthu. Fuckin' weekend warriors. Apparently, they were called up by the satraps' local underlings—called vavasors—but hadn't

shown much enthusiasm for taking on the Clarthuuns or the Kedlakis until they got the gear from the Hardliners."

"Tang?"

Jackson snorted. "Space OJ?"

"Nnnmmm. Traneng," Chalmers said carefully.

"Training?" Jackson asked.

Chalmers didn't answer, fully occupied with suppressing a resur-
gence of the itch.

"I'm just gonna take your trembling for a yes. We're still trying to
run that down, but it looks like some of the satrapies allow locals to
guest-train on the equipment they keep stored in their city armories.
We couldn't ask questions of the mortar men, for reasons you know
already. The rest either got away or got themselves executed by the
Clarthuuns, who were straight *pissed*. Oh, and in case you're wondering where we are that I'm able to knock back Wild Turkey like the
good ole days, then wonder no more: we're in the new camp. All of
us. The Kedlakis-Ur and her people came, too, once they heard from
Ked that vengeance had been taken for the affront to her niece—
that'd be the little badass, Kenla—and we'd settled the rest of the
matter for them."

Chalmers stirred.

"And about the scores getting settled? Apparently that was part
of the plan from the get-go. At least, according to the Kedlakis-Ur.
The village hetman's kid, the one Kenla killed? He wanted to take
over from his pops but had been refused by the village council. So,
he gets all angry and shit, and starts shopping the village to the,
uh...the vavasors. Real dirtbag, this fucker.

"Somewhere along the line, a vavasor puts him in touch with the
local satrap's fixer, who hooks him up with those RPGs. It was part
of a deal to not only get control of the village, but as many of the
nomads as he could convince to come over to their side. And, get

this! He apparently approached the Kedlakis-Ur's niece to negotiate a deal that would betray us all to the satrap. When the niece told him to pound salt, he attacked her."

Another pull on the bottle, then a bourbon-rasped, "I remember thinking, given how easy she was about dueling the hetman and *controlling* that fight to buy us time, that his rat-fuck son must have had a trick up his sleeve to even think about attacking Kenla himself. Didn't make sense at the time, but then enter the drug the healer used to put me down."

Jackson coughed. Another slosh. Chalmers heard the bottle thump on the ground.

"So...so then. What am I missing?" Jackson's slur was fairly strong now. "So...so the healer, right? She's pissed about her son—oh, yeah, the healer and the hetman were a couple back when. But she'd made her peace with the break-up. She wasn't happy about her boy making deals with the enemy and then stealing her drugs to mickey the Kedlakis-Ur's niece. Oh, no, not the kind of shit a wise woman or whatever can take lying down. Goes against her oaths and whatnot. So she's pissed, right? But it's her kid, right? So, she decides to get rid of the evidence that shows he's working for the wrong side...and that's when we show up and I put a round in her chest." Chalmers heard Jackson's hands scrubbing the stubble of his cheeks. "Fuck, me, but I'm glad I didn't kill her..."

Silence settled around them.

Chalmers wasn't sure he understood all of it, or that it all made sense, but what he did comprehend jibed with the behaviors he'd seen from the principal players in this little intertribal drama.

"Cmmn?" he asked.

"Common?"

Chalmers nodded.

"I'm afraid I don't understand you, Chalmers. Maybe if I take that off." Chalmers heard a *thump*, like the front pair of a chair's legs hitting a wood floor after someone leaning back came fully forward. A clinking, as of scissors being taken off an aluminum tray, then, "Hold still."

Chalmers, helpless to do anything but, did as he was told. A few seconds later he was blinking into a lantern hung from one of the tent's supports while Jackson got rid of the remaining bandages that had swaddled his head so tightly he couldn't speak.

Jackson sat, returned his chair to the preferred angle of lean with his boots on Chalmers' bed, and allowed a big shit-eating grin to slowly spread across his face.

"What?" Chalmers asked. Surprised at the lack of pain, he tried to raise an arm to touch his face and survey the damage, but Jackson hadn't cut his hands free.

"Nothin'," Jackson slurred.

"Wait, why am I feeling no pain?"

"'Cause you're in heaven?" Jackson ventured, fixing Chalmers with a leer.

"Fuck you. We both know I'm going to hell when I die." He blinked, struggling to get his hands free, still feeling no pain—at least from his face, despite talking. "Wait, why was my jaw tied up?"

"Already told you. I wanted to get a word in edgewise."

"Jackson!" Chalmers shouted, the deep breath that followed and the struggle to get his arms free causing a harsh throb from deep beneath his ribs.

Jackson laughed, hiccupped.

"What the fuck, Jackson?" Chalmers wheezed.

"You like that shit? I'm particularly proud of the alien fungus bit I came up with, though I think I might have over-sold the cracker shit Sonningen wanted to act out." He looked a question at Chalmers.

"B-b-but, you said I was out for weeks?"

"Jesus, man!" Jackson snorted, waving a dismissive hand. "You just lost a shit-ton of blood, had some deep lacerations, and broke two ribs. The crazy drugs they have here did for the lacerations, and you're wrapped pretty tight around the chest. The face wounds are already pinked scars. You've only been out...uh, a little less than two days, I think." He paused, thinking. "Yeah, two days. Shit did really get fuzzy at the end, there."

"Wait, so no alien fungus?" Chalmers asked, bewildered.

Jackson laughed. "Fuck no!"

"Untie me, then, you asshole!" The shout drove a spike of pain through his ribs. Chalmers decided not to shout, ever again.

Jackson only laughed harder as he watched Chalmers' face contort. "Nah," he eventually gasped, wiping at tears, "I think I'm gonna enjoy this a while longer." He reached down and plucked the bottle from the ground. Saluting Chalmers with it, he took a long swig, swallowed, and said, "Not every day I get to shut you up at will."

Jackson made a face as the liquor went down. Now calm enough to note the bottle wasn't Wild Turkey, but some of the local rotgut, Chalmers let go of his earlier jealousy.

He also didn't repeat himself. Didn't beg. Now that his temper had cooled, Chalmers knew better. Old Chalmers might have begged. More likely he'd have raged and cursed. But new Chalmers wasn't about to beg. Not that Jackson wouldn't accede to a properly worded beg-fest, but because that was exactly what Jackson wanted.

No, Chalmers' choice was about himself. New Chalmers had, ultimately, been better. Done better. He'd sacrificed his body to save Jackson from injury, and they both knew it.

The whole purpose of Jackson's charade was to distract them both from the changes wrought on their relationship by surviving the shit-show together. They both knew their lives had rested in the other's hands in ways they never had before, that whatever sins Chalmers had committed in the past, they were just that, in the past, and he had done better with his present.

Against all previous experience and expectation, Chalmers had made good on some of the oaths he'd sworn, both to himself and to Jackson.

Neither of them could acknowledge what they had done for each other, not openly. To do so would break the unspoken contract. Jackson had come close to breaking it back in Kedlakis, but he'd been justified. Anger and honor wore a completely different set of responsibilities than gratitude, and it demanded a different set of rules. Gratitude was not to be spoken of, not to be displayed. Not between them.

So instead they would continue this complicated dance, neither admitting to the other exactly what the other meant to them until one or the other was dead.

And that was fine by both new and old Chalmers.

Really.

"Can I get a sip, Jacks?"

"Sure, sure," Jackson said, holding the bottle out to his partner.

Chalmers reached, but his hands were still tied.

Jackson fell out of his chair laughing.

# # # # #

# ABOUT THE AUTHOR

Griffin spent his youth in four different countries, learning three languages, and burning all his bridges. Finally settled in Northern California with a day job as a police officer in a major metropolitan department, he lives the good life with his lovely wife, crazy-smart daughter, and needy dog. 1636: Mission to the Mughals, co-authored with Eric Flint, was his first novel. He's written a number of shorts for various anthologies including Chuck Gannon's Lost Signals. Second Chance Angel, co-authored with Kacey Ezell, is forthcoming in September.

\* \* \* \* \*

## The Caine Riordan Universe

The Caine Riordan series and Terran Republic universe deliver gritty yet doggedly optimistic hard scifi in a world that is a believable and embattled successor to our own. For those who are not familiar with the series' hallmark blend of exploration, alien encounters, intrigue, and action, you can find them all right here:

The **Caine Riordan** series
(Baen Books)
*Fire with Fire*
*Trial by Fire*
*Raising Caine*
*Caine's Mutiny*
*Marque of Caine*
*Endangered Species* (forthcoming)
*Protected Species* (forthcoming)
*Triage* (forthcoming, with Eric Flint)

The **Murphy's Lawless** series
*Shakes*
*Obligations*
*Man-Eater*
*Promises* (coming June 17, 2020)

Other works in the **Terran Republic** universe
*Lost Signals* (Ring of Fire Press)

Since that list includes a winner of the Compton Crook Award, four Nebula finalists, and two Dragon finalists, they're not hard to find. Just go wherever books are sold. Want to learn more about the Caine Riordan series? Easy. Contact any of the publishers, or you can reach out to me at contact@charlesegannon.com.

Want to see more of what's going on in the Terran Republic universe? Check out http://www.charlesegannon.com for exclusive written and visual content.

And if you decide you don't want to miss a single new release or announcement, then go to http://charlesegannon.com/wp/sign-up/ to join the all-inclusive mailing list for sneak peeks, special offers, and features you won't see anywhere else.

And most important of all…welcome aboard; we're glad you're here!

The following is an

**Excerpt from Book One of the Revelations Cycle:**

# Cartwright's Cavaliers

---

# Mark Wandrey

Available Now from Seventh Seal Press

eBook, Paperback, and Audio Book

**Excerpt from "Cartwright's Cavaliers:"**

The last two operational tanks were trapped on their chosen path. Faced with destroyed vehicles front and back, they cut sideways to the edge of the dry river bed they'd been moving along and found several large boulders to maneuver around that allowed them to present a hull-down defensive position. Their troopers rallied on that position. It was starting to look like they'd dig in when Phoenix 1 screamed over and strafed them with dual streams of railgun rounds. A split second later, Phoenix 2 followed on a parallel path. Jim was just cheering the air attack when he saw it. The sixth damned tank, and it was a heavy.

"I got that last tank," Jim said over the command net.

"Observe and stand by," Murdock said.

"We'll have these in hand shortly," Buddha agreed, his transmission interspersed with the thudding of his CASPer firing its magnet accelerator. "We can be there in a few minutes."

Jim examined his battlespace. The tank was massive. It had to be one of the fusion-powered beasts he'd read about. Which meant shields and energy weapons. It was heading down the same gap the APC had taken, so it was heading toward Second Squad, and fast.

"Shit," he said.

"Jim," Hargrave said, "we're in position. What are you doing?"

"Leading," Jim said as he jumped out from the rock wall.

\* \* \* \* \*

Get "Cartwright's Cavaliers" now at:
https://www.amazon.com/dp/B01MRZKM95

Find out more about Mark Wandrey and the Four Horsemen Universe at:

https://chriskennedypublishing.com/the-four-horsemen-books/

\* \* \* \* \*

The following is an

**Excerpt from Book One of the Salvage Title Trilogy:**

# Salvage Title

---

# Kevin Steverson

Available Now from Theogony Books

eBook, Paperback, and Audio Book

**Excerpt from "Salvage Title:"**

The first thing Clip did was get power to the door and the access panel. Two of his power cells did the trick once he had them wired to the container. He then pulled out his slate and connected it. It lit up, and his fingers flew across it. It took him a few minutes to establish a link, then he programmed it to search for the combination to the access panel.

"Is it from a human ship?" Harmon asked, curious.

"I don't think so, but it doesn't matter; ones and zeros are still ones and zeros when it comes to computers. It's universal. I mean, there are some things you have to know to get other races' computers to run right, but it's not that hard," Clip said.

Harmon shook his head. *Riiigghht,* he thought. He knew better. Clip's intelligence test results were completely off the charts. Clip opted to go to work at Rinto's right after secondary school because there was nothing for him to learn at the colleges and universities on either Tretra or Joth. He could have received academic scholarships for advanced degrees on a number of nearby systems. He could have even gone all the way to Earth and attended the University of Georgia if he wanted. The problem was getting there. The schools would have provided free tuition if he could just have paid to get there.

Secondary school had been rough on Clip. He was a small guy that made excellent grades without trying. It would have been worse if Harmon hadn't let everyone know that Clip was his brother. They lived in the same foster center, so it was mostly true. The first day of school, Harmon had laid down the law—if you messed with Clip, you messed up.

At the age of fourteen, he beat three seniors senseless for attempting to put Clip in a trash container. One of them was a Yalteen, a member of a race of large humanoids from two systems over. It wasn't a fair fight—they should have brought more people with them. Harmon hated bullies.

133

After the suspension ended, the school's Warball coach came to see him. He started that season as a freshman and worked on using it to earn a scholarship to the academy. By the time he graduated, he was six feet two inches with two hundred and twenty pounds of muscle. He got the scholarship and a shot at going into space. It was the longest time he'd ever spent away from his foster brother, but he couldn't turn it down.

Clip stayed on Joth and went to work for Rinto. He figured it was a job that would get him access to all kinds of technical stuff, servos, motors, and maybe even some alien computers. The first week he was there, he tweaked the equipment and increased the plant's recycled steel production by 12 percent. Rinto was eternally grateful, as it put him solidly into the profit column instead of toeing the line between profit and loss. When Harmon came back to the planet after the academy, Rinto hired him on the spot on Clip's recommendation. After he saw Harmon operate the grappler and got to know him, he was glad he did.

A steady beeping brought Harmon back to the present. Clip's program had succeeded in unlocking the container. "Right on!" Clip exclaimed. He was always using expressions hundreds or more years out of style. "Let's see what we have; I hope this one isn't empty, too." Last month they'd come across a smaller vault, but it had been empty.

Harmon stepped up and wedged his hands into the small opening the door had made when it disengaged the locks. There wasn't enough power in the small cells Clip used to open it any further. He put his weight into it, and the door opened enough for them to get inside. Before they went in, Harmon placed a piece of pipe in the doorway so it couldn't close and lock on them, baking them alive before anyone realized they were missing.

Daylight shone in through the doorway, and they both froze in place; the weapons vault was full.

\* \* \* \* \*

Get "Salvage Title" now at:
https://www.amazon.com/dp/B07H8Q3HBV.

Find out more about Kevin Steverson and "Salvage Title" at:
http://chriskennedypublishing.com/.

\* \* \* \* \*

The following is an

**Excerpt from Book One of The Progenitors' War:**

# A Gulf in Time

---

# Chris Kennedy

Available from Theogony Books

eBook, Paperback, and (Soon) Audio

**Excerpt from "A Gulf in Time:"**

"Thank you for calling us," the figure on the front view screen said, his pupil-less eyes glowing bright yellow beneath his eight-inch horns. Generally humanoid, the creature was blood red and had a mouthful of pointed teeth that were visible when he smiled. Giant bat wings alternately spread and folded behind him; his pointed tail could be seen flicking back and forth when the wings were folded. "We accept your offer to be our slaves for now and all eternity."

"Get us out of here, helm!" Captain Sheppard ordered. "Flank speed to the stargate!"

"Sorry, sir, my console is dead," the helmsman replied.

"Can you jump us to the Jinn Universe?"

"No, sir, that's dead too."

"Engineer, do we have our shields?"

"No, sir, they're down, and my console's dead, too."

"OSO? DSO? Status?"

"My console's dead," the Offensive Systems Officer replied.

"Mine, too," the Defensive Systems Officer noted.

The figure on the view screen laughed. "I do *so* love the way new minions scamper about, trying to avoid the unavoidable."

"There's been a mistake," Captain Sheppard said. "We didn't intend to call you or become your minions."

"It does not matter whether you *intended* to or not," the creature said. "You passed the test and are obviously strong enough to function as our messengers."

"What do you mean, 'to function as your messengers?'"

"It is past time for this galaxy's harvest. You will go to all the civilizations and prepare them for the cull."

"I'm not sure I like the sound of that. What is this 'cull?'"

"We require your life force in order to survive. Each civilization will be required to provide 98.2% of its life force. The remaining 1.8% will be used to reseed their planets."

"And you expect us to take this message to all the civilized planets in this galaxy?"

"That is correct. Why else would we have left the stargates for you to use to travel between the stars?"

"What if a civilization doesn't want to participate in this cull?"

"Then they will be obliterated. Most will choose to save 1.8% of their population, rather than none, especially once you make an example or two of the civilizations who refuse."

"And if *we* refuse?"

"Then your society will be the first example."

"I can't make this kind of decision," Captain Sheppard said, stalling. "I'll have to discuss it with my superiors."

"Unacceptable. You must give me an answer now. Kneel before us or perish; those are your choices."

"I can't," Captain Sheppard said, his voice full of anguish.

"Who called us by completing the quest?" the creature asked. "That person must decide."

"I pushed the button," Lieutenant Commander Hobbs replied, "but I can't commit my race to this any more than Captain Sheppard can."

"That is all right," the creature said. "Sometimes it is best to have an example from the start." He looked off screen. "Destroy them."

"Captain Sheppard, there are energy weapons warming up on the other ship," Steropes said.

"DSO, now would be a good time for those shields…" Captain Sheppard said.

"I'm sorry, sir; my console is still dead."

"They're firing!" Steropes called.

The enemy ship fired, but the *Vella Gulf*'s shields snapped on, absorbing the volley.

"Nice job, DSO!" Captain Sheppard exclaimed.

"I didn't do it, sir!" the DSO cried. "They just came on."

"Well, if you didn't do it, who did?" Captain Sheppard asked.

"I don't know!" the DSO exclaimed. "All I know is we can't take another volley like that, sir; the first round completely maxed out our shields. One more, and they're going to fail!"

"I...activated...the shields," Solomon, the ship's artificial intelligence, said. The voice of the AI sounded strained. "Am fighting...intruder..." the AI's voice fluctuated between male and female. "Losing...system...integrity...krelbet gelched."

"Krelbet gelched?" the DSO asked.

"It means 'systems failing' in the language of the Eldive," Steropes said.

"The enemy is firing again," the DSO said. "We're hit! Shields are down."

"I've got hits down the length of the ship," the duty engineer said. "We're open to space in several places. We can't take another round like that!"

"That was just the little that came through after the shields fell," the DSO said. "We're doomed if—*missiles inbound!* I've got over 100 missiles inbound, and I can't do anything to stop them!" He switched to the public address system. "*Numerous missiles inbound! All hands brace for shock!* Five seconds! Three...two...one..."

\* \* \* \* \*

Get "A Gulf in Time" now at:
https://www.amazon.com/dp/B0829FLV92

Find out more about Chris Kennedy and "A Gulf in Time" at:
https://chriskennedypublishing.com/imprints-authors/chris-kennedy/

\* \* \* \* \*

Made in the USA
Middletown, DE
28 June 2020

10488221R00080